HARD TIMES

John Hansen

HARD TIMES
Published through SUMMIT CREEK PRESS

*To my wife Debi whose patience and support
made this book possible.*

This is a work of fiction. Names, characters, places, and incidents are the product of the author's imagination or are used fictitiously. Any resemblance to actual persons, living or dead, events, or locales is entirely coincidental.

All rights reserved
Copyright © 2019 by John Hansen
Cover art copyright © 2019 by
http://www.selfpubbookcovers.com/Zendesign

ISBN: 978-0-578-45823-6

No part of this publication may be reproduced, stored in a retrieval system, or transmitted in any form or by any means electronic, mechanical, photocopying, recording, or otherwise, without the written permission of the author or publisher.

CHAPTER ONE

Phil Caldwell turned his fork on edge and carved out a good sized bite of sourdough hotcake that had been smothered with butter and chokecherry syrup. He then speared it and brushed it under his bushy black moustache into his mouth and chewed a few times before looking across the table at his wife, Martha. "It's ah helluva note," he said as he reached for his coffee cup. "Havin' ta go forty-two feet ta find water."

Martha looked annoyed. "Count your blessings, Phillip. Just think of all the folks hereabouts that have come up with dusters."

Phil knew that Martha wanted to be done digging the well just as much as he did but, for whatever reason, she'd gotten to where she wouldn't tolerate his grousing even if it was mostly to break the silence in their tiny one room shack. He adjusted his tenor to be more positive and looked straight into her blue eyes so she would know he meant well. "I was standin' in ah good three inches ah water yesterday when we quit. With any luck at all, we could have six inches this mornin'."

Martha scoffed as if Phil was being overly naïve. "Even if you're right, what difference will it make? It wouldn't matter if there was six feet of water in the bottom of that hole – it's not enough to irrigate our crops."

"Maybe not but we can save the garden."

Martha laughed "Why yes, Phillip, we can take a sack of potatoes to the bank this fall. I'm sure that will satisfy our note."

"If it rains we'll be all right."

"Ever body 'round here is hopin' an' prayin' for rain. Another ten days and we'll be into July. The wheat will be dead by then."

Phil reckoned he was somewhere in between a 'hope-er' and a 'pray-er' as deep down he put the chances of rain coming on par with rolling dice for drinks at the Rosebud Saloon in town. He seldom won. Nonetheless he wouldn't allow himself to go where Martha was and forced a smile. "Just think, when we git the well done there'll be no more haulin' water. Why, I been thinkin' since the well is up slope from the house I could build a cistern up there, fill it and gravity feed the water right down here."

Martha appeared unimpressed. Her demeanor was more like she was indulging him so as to not be outright mean spirited. Still, she could not help herself. "We had a good life in Lincoln."

Phil came back quick, unable to hide the anger in his voice. "For you maybe."

Martha paused, knowing how Phil hated his job at the flour mill. She was reluctant to go on but then she did. "We had a house with running water, electricity and even a telephone. We had neighbors. There were people to talk to just about whenever you wanted. It's lonely here, Phillip, and the wind, the damned wind, it never stops." And then she suddenly went quiet, realizing perhaps that she'd heaped a lot on his plate.

The smile, the hopefulness in Phil's eyes went away. He ran his right hand through his short dark hair and looked down at the red and white checkered oilcloth that covered the table. He remembered how pleased Martha had been the day they had bought it in town. Things had been different then. There'd been no drought and the expectation that life would be good was believable. But now mother-nature, God, chance, wherever a person chose to lay the blame had gutted those expectations. Phil looked off to his right and their bed pushed against the wall. The drought had extended to there as well, until last night. It had been good for him but he was uncertain about her. She seemed to be somewhere else.

Martha slid her wooden chair back on the rough plank floor and started toward the wood burning stove behind her. "You want some more coffee?"

Phil looked up. "Yeah, I'll take a cup." He took Martha's offer of coffee as a sign she was through venting, or at least he hoped so, as the guilt he felt in having brought her here to homestead handicapped him in any kind of debate about the rightness or wrongness of it all.

The stove was still burning hot, cracking and popping, causing the metal coffee pot sitting on it to purr. Martha took a pot holder from the shelf above the stove and brought the pot back to the table, filling first Phil's cup and then hers.

Phil reached for his coffee. "Thanks."

Martha thought to smile but it could not penetrate the layer of worry that gripped her face. Instead, a sense of awkwardness came over her like her inner feelings were being exposed. It was like she was in a dressing room and the curtain had been suddenly yanked open. Her eyes caught

Phil's for just a moment before she turned and put the pot back on the stove.

Phil stared at Martha's long auburn hair. She'd done it up in a French braid. It was one of the things that had drawn him to her nearly twenty years ago. She'd not changed much over the years. There were the beginnings of crow's feet at the corners of her eyes but she was still pretty and shapely, maybe due to the fact that she'd never had kids. At five foot five she was about a head shorter than him. As Martha returned to the table, he said, "You know they got that moving picture place in town now. Maybe Saturday night we could go to the show."

"We don't have the money for that, do we?"

"We'll manage. It'll be our reward for finishing the well."

Martha became mute. Seconds began to tick by. Mere seconds, but already she could see the effect of her hesitation in Phil's eyes. The excitement, the anticipation of what could be, was fading from them like life from a dying man. Finally, she said: "Sure Honey, that sounds swell."

Phil wanted to scream at her, *What's wrong with you? Where's the old Martha?* But he did not. He continued the façade. "We'll have a grand time. Maybe have supper at the diner before we go to the theater, but we'll leave room for some popcorn and lemonade while we watch the picture show."

Martha did her best to manufacture a smile. "It'll be fun, I'm sure."

Phil tried to ignore the uneasiness between them and moved on lest Martha allow the silence to return. Looking beyond her and to the left of the stove at a vacant spot on the wall beneath some shelves that contained canned goods, dishes and such, he said, "If I git water piped down here I'll put ya ah sink right there."

Martha glanced over to where Phil was looking. "That'd be nice."

"Oh, don't ya know it. I could pipe the wastewater outside too. Be just like back in Lincoln."

"We'd be just like town folks," replied Martha in a tone that bordered on patronizing.

Phil paused and took several long sips of coffee, all the while trying to gauge why Martha was being the way she was. At first he felt foolish for attempting to put a good spin on how life could be for them there amongst the endless coulees and buttes of southeastern Montana, but then he became agitated when her body language made it clear that she didn't care about the sink and running water. Without speaking he pushed his chair back, stood and moved to the window behind him. He parted the pale yellow curtains that she had made and looked through the flyspecked glass as if there was a reason he needed to. He took another drink of coffee, still staring out the window. For a time neither of them spoke, their tongues seemingly held at bay by the sirens of loneliness; the fire cracking and popping in the stove, the alarm clock on the shelf above Phil's head ticking away and outside a Meadowlark whistling its melodic song.

At last she said, "Maybe we should get started on the well. Didn't you say Jack Schneider was coming this afternoon to help cement around the opening of it?"

From the corner of his eye Phil could see the wood box to the left of the door. It was made of rough boards and measured four feet square by three feet high. It was nearly empty. Thinking Martha would appreciate the delay in having to stand at the windlass over the well opening and winch buckets of gravel up, he said, "Why don't I fill the wood box before we start back on the well?"

"No, let's just get busy. It's already seven minutes past eight. We should've been working by now."

Phil turned around and glared at Martha for just an instant and then set his coffee cup on the table next to his plate with the partially eaten hotcake. "All right, I'll be down the well. You come when yer ready."

"I'll be along shortly," she said as if she was oblivious to the tension between them.

Phil paused at the door to retrieve his black felt hat from one of the nails he'd driven in the wall there. He thought to say, even wanted to say, something nice like; *Thanks for breakfast. It was real good.* But he couldn't bring himself to do it so he left things as they were and went outside where he was immediately set upon by their mongrel dog, Ranger, wanting to play. Phil reached down and ruffled the dog's ears. "Hey Ranger dog. What are you doin'? Are you ready to go to the well? Huh. Well, let's go." And so they set off up the deep, tall grass coulee that was maybe 300 yards wide at this point, but went on for a good mile or so before it pinched shut and rose up to a big flat mesa where a person could still find buffalo bones littering the ground. The well, however, was about 100 yards north of their shack. Too far, in Phil's opinion, to tote water but the shack had come first and the water witcher second. *Right here's the spot*, he had declared so Phil went to digging. There would, after all, have been no point in him paying the man to come from clear on the other side of Baker to witch the well if he was going to dispute its location.

About fifteen feet from the windlass was a sizeable pile of dirt and rock where Martha had been emptying the buckets that she had cranked up. She'd concentrated the dirt, like Phil had instructed her, in one place so as to not smother the grass over a large area. It was hard work for Martha. She weighed about 115 pounds. The dirt bucket was made of tin and would hold five gallons of water. When filled with dirt and rock it would be approaching about half her weight. Phil had just started reattaching the bucket to the end of the rope that was wound around the axel of the windlass when Ranger suddenly bolted away down the path they'd worn to the house. Phil's eyes followed Ranger to see that Martha had just rounded the corner of their shanty and was coming up the coulee. In that instant, seeing her next to their little shack with its tarpaper covered roof caused guilt to wash over him for having taken her away from the finer things in Lincoln. It was a feeling, however, that was never far from his mind since having staked their homestead.

The bucket had just about reached the bottom of the well when, from behind him came Martha's voice, "I was on my way."

Phil paused and glanced back at her. "I know. Figured you had things to do." He went back to unwinding the rope with the bucket until he heard it splash in the water. "Ya hear that? Sounds like a good amount ah water down there."

"It does, Phillip. It surely does."

Phil had worn knee-high rubber boots today to keep his feet dry while mucking out the mud at the bottom of the well. He laughed and then said jokingly, "Why hells-bells, maybe I shudda wore my swimmin' trunks." And then he laughed some more.

Martha barely grinned, even though she could see that Phil was watching for her response. It was as if her facial muscles were the consistency of cold taffy and just wouldn't give way to a smile let alone laughter. She came back, mostly business-like, "I'm happy for you, Phillip. It looks to be a good well, but we should get it finished."

It was hard for Phil to not take offense at Martha's demeanor. She wasn't being exactly rude but, if her behavior could be equated to standing near the edge of a cliff, he was certain that it'd scare the hell out of most men. Reluctantly, he turned away from her and picked up the end of a coiled rope lying on the ground near the opening of the well. It was an inch in diameter and knotted about every four feet. He'd borrowed it from a neighbor who had dug a well last year. After tying the rope to the axel of the windlass, he gathered the rest of it from the ground and dropped it down the well. He stared down the hole after the rope, heard it splash, but couldn't see the water for the darkness. "Stands to reason," he began while poised over the hole, "that I ain't gonna be able to work very long if we got much water. It gits ta be crotch deep and I'm comin' up." Phil paused, grinning and thinking he'd add some cute remark about, *not wanting to damage his privates in the cold water,* but before he could put that out there Martha chimed in apparently indifferent to where he was hinting at going. "Just make sure it's plenty deep enough, Phillip. I don't want to have to come back out here at some later date on account of the well going dry."

Before he could catch himself, Phil shot Martha a dirty look. "Trust me, after today I got no desire to ever again go down this hole."

"I'm sorry, Phillip. I didn't mean to be bossy."

Phil ignored her apology and took hold of the knotted rope. If things had been better between them this morning he would have given her a kiss and told her that he loved her as hand dug wells sometimes caved in. Instead, as he started down the rope, he said in a business like tone, "I'll holler when I git to the bottom."

"Okay, I'll pull the rope up then."

Phil took a deep breath and exhaled as if to push the uneasiness between them from his mind. There would be no room for it going down the rope. He needed to concentrate. With his leather gloves on he gripped the bristly hemp tight to start with, and then alternated relaxing his grip and sliding down to a knot where he would unclasp his feet, reposition them below that knot before sliding on to the next one. It was cumbersome going down but the knots provided plenty of rest stops climbing up. Starting out, when there was sufficient light, he could see roots protruding from the earth surrounding him, but within five or six feet the roots ended. The soil changed too from being mostly silty and rich to gravelly. And then, at about 25 feet, the light became so poor he had only an awareness of the soil being there due mostly to its musty smell. But on he went, going deeper into the ground until at last his feet touched water causing him to gasp slightly and tighten his grip on the rope so he would come to a stop. He then proceeded to slowly lower himself into the water. It was a strange feeling, a scary feeling to be doing this in the bottom of a black hole. There seemed to be no end to it when suddenly his feet hit solid ground. The well had done better than he thought. The water was within about three inches of going over the tops of his knee high rubber boots. He took his hat off and leaned back so he could look straight up. Far away through the molasses of darkness was a pinhole of light. He could just make out Martha peering down into the oblivion of the well. For a moment, he became claustrophobic. His heart began to race and his lungs felt like they were being gripped by some unseen force. And in his mind's eye images of his old life in Lincoln taunted him with blue skies and sunshine. He wanted, at that very moment, to just call the well '*good enough*' and climb the knotted rope back to the light and life but Martha's words still echoed, if not stung in their correctness, to make sure the well was *plenty deep enough.* "Damn her," he whispered aloud. And then he collected himself. Cupping his right hand to the side of his mouth he shouted up at her, "You can pull the rope up now."

Although Martha had called out in a loud voice, "Okay", it sounded to Phil almost like he had a pillow over his head. Nonetheless, the knotted rope started to move, decluttering the bottom of the hole of its eight extra feet. Still, it was cozy with the dirt bucket and him at five foot ten trying to manage a long handled shovel in a space that was roughly four and a half feet square.

Phil sighed as he began probing his shirt pocket for a small cardboard box of stick matches. Finding it, he held the box in the darkness before him and carefully felt of it to make sure it was right side up. He then gently removed a match and lit it on the side of the box. The yellow flame illuminated a gas lantern hanging from a steel peg that he had driven into the earthen wall. Shielding the match with one hand he moved it quickly to the lantern and brought light to his situation. The shovel was leaning in the corner to the right of the lantern. The metal bucket, however, had already sunk. It was clear to him that he'd be working blind, digging and filling the bucket under water. *This shouldn't take too long,* he said to himself. *It can't with the water being what it is.* Rolling up the sleeves of his shirt, he reached into the cold water and set the bucket upright. He was glad that he'd worn his rubber boots today as the water temperature suggested it could be painful if a person was to be exposed to it for very long. Grabbing up the shovel, he began to dig. Within a minute or so it became apparent to him that shoveling mud under water required patience, as moving the shovel too fast would wash some or all of your load off. The other realization that came to him after the third bucket was that, as he deepened his little swimming hole, his rubber boots were no longer tall enough and the water's effects were as he'd imagined they would be.

"Take her up, Martha."

"All right." The bucket began its ascent with a sudden jerk followed by a smooth lift for about a foot before slowing almost to a stop as Martha struggled to push the crank of the windlass to its highest point, which was just about beyond her reach, and then the bucket picked up speed again as she put her weight into it on the down turn. Due to her size, it was a slow laborious task for her that got no better once the bucket came out of the well, as then it was suspended over the center of the open hole. It was here that she had to step out on a plank and disconnect the bucket and carry it with both hands to the dirt pile. It was little wonder that she preferred life in Lincoln.

It had been several minutes since Martha had unhooked the bucket. Phil was leaning against the dirt wall opposite the lantern puffing on a Lucky Strike cigarette when he heard Martha shout, "I'll be back in a minute. There's an automobile coming to the house."

It took maybe three or four seconds for it to register with Phil what Martha had said and for him to pluck the cigarette from his mouth and tilt his head back so he could direct his shout up to her. "Send the bucket back down. Ah coupla more will finish it." But he was talking to the sky mostly as he caught just a glimpse of her blue gingham dress swirling away from the opening. After a minute or so of staring up at the light of day waiting for her to return with the bucket, the realization that she either hadn't heard him or had chosen to ignore him sunk in. "Well shit," he said aloud. "I guess I'll just stand here and twiddle my thumbs until she's done passin' the time ah day with whoever has come to the house. Probably some damned drummer pedaling crap we ain't got the money to buy."

Martha's sudden departure caused a ripple of anger and panic within Phil. "Damn her. I don't know why she didn't lower the bucket. Another half hour an' we could be done." He took the last drag off of his cigarette and then expelled the blue-gray smoke out into the damp air before him. It hung there for the longest time, in the light of the lantern refusing to dissipate in the stillness. He crushed the cigarette butt against the wall of the well and put it in his shirt pocket. And then he just stood there and listened and listened and listened for Martha's return. But there was nothing but the hissing and sputtering of the gas lantern. Its sound was both a curse and a comfort. Like a bubbling cauldron, the fear within him suddenly boiled over. He whimpered, "Where can she be? She knows I'm down here." And then he looked up at the light above that seemed so far away and yelled as loud as he could, "Martha. Martha…" over and over until finally he sank back against the wall of the well and took what solace he could from the noise and light of the lantern. His heart was pounding. He was afraid not only for himself but for Martha. "What could've happened to her?" He checked his pocket watch. "Twenty minutes past nine," he whispered. Time was a formidable adversary. The water had risen now so that even standing on the highest spot he could find it poured into his boots. His feet and legs up to his knees were cold. He looked at his watch again and visually followed the Roman numerals from nine around to one. He shook his head. "Oh please Jack, be on time." And then the fear swept over him again like the tide was coming in and he'd been caught off guard. He replayed, as best he could recall, Martha's last words to him hoping there was some clue in them as to who might have come to the house. But they were just plain words that suggested nothing, leaving him to speculate and fear the worst. And the silence, save for the hissing of the lantern returned.

It was an effort, a conscious effort to keep fear at bay. It would have already won out had it not been for the hope that Jack Schneider would be there at one o'clock to help build forms and pour cement. At ten minutes till one, Phil began to feel a sense of relief. *Jacks's a responsible guy. Hell, he's almost 40, got ah wife and two kids. He'll be here.* He'd visualized again and again Jack, a big guy with dark eyes and moustache, coming up the path from the house and rescuing him from the well. The vision was so clear he felt guilty at feeling such an upsurge in his spirits knowing that he would soon be out of the well, while not knowing what had happened to Martha. But this feeling was short-lived as the prospect of dying in the well pushed it out of his mind. And then one o'clock came and went. It was a quarter past one and Jack still hadn't come. Suddenly, it occurred to him that maybe Jack was at the house. Panic seized Phil like he'd never felt in his life. *What if Jack looked up towards the well and not seeing me just assumed, since no one is at the house, that I forgot about today and both me and Martha went somewhere with somebody.* Frantically, he began to scream Jack's name as loud as he could. *Jack, I'm up here. I'm in the well. Jack. Jack.* He went on like this until he was hoarse and his head was throbbing. He was cold and exhausted. The tears that had formed in his eyes now broke free. They began to cascade down his cheeks. "Oh God," he sobbed, "Please help me. Don't let me die here." Phil was not religious in the sense of go to church on Sunday and pay your tithe kind of guy, but he believed in a higher power and that there was an existence after death. Just what form that existence took he wasn't certain, but he was desperate and needed to believe there was some greater goodness that would rescue him as it was clear that Jack wasn't coming. Suddenly, a dog's bark sounded above him. He instantly looked up. Ranger had walked out onto the plank that straddled the well opening beneath the windlass and was looking down into the darkness. Phil began shouting up to the dog, fearful that he would leave without understanding that he was in the well. "Ranger, I'm down here. What a good dog you are. I need help Ranger. Is Martha at the house? Can you go get her?"

Ranger began barking more but there was no sign of Jack or Martha coming because of it. The closest neighbor was a single woman. Her shack was a little over a mile away and even if she heard Ranger she would probably think he was barking at birds or prairie dogs. And then it became a moot point as Ranger laid down on the plank and went silent. At first glance Phil was afraid that he'd left, but then he could see about three inches of one of Ranger's hind legs extending off of the plank. It gave him reason for hope knowing that he wasn't alone, even if it was just Ranger.

The day wore on. It was not as bright up above as it had been. Phil checked his watch. It was twenty minutes till three. His legs ached from having stood in the cold water for so long. He wanted badly to be free of it and to lie down in the light of day where it was warm and dry and he could see the sky from horizon to horizon and sleep. And he wanted to know too what had happened to Martha. And he regretted not eating all of his hotcakes that morning. He had passed the time by checking frequently to make sure that Ranger was still on the plank and noting the time. And then suddenly the lantern began to sputter and hesitate and the bright yellow flame died away to just the glowing red mesh of the lantern's mantle. Phil stared at the tiny glowing jewels in the darkness until they winked out. Almost right away he felt more alone and destined to die there. He likened himself to a mouse that falls in a well. It swims round and round searching desperately for an escape until finally its muscles give in to fatigue and it sinks below the surface. It tries in vain to not breathe in the water but the pain is too great. Death does not come easy for it. The water now is up to Phil's crotch. It is no joking matter as it had been that morning. His legs are so stiff he can hardly move them. "Ah dammit," he groaned. "If I could just git outta this water." Somewhere in the darkness to his right the shovel is leaning against the wall of the well. Like a blind man he made a slow sweeping gesture with his hand until he touched it. Grabbing hold of it, he pulled it toward him to where he could overlay the palms of his hands on the top of the shovel's handle allowing it to take some of the weight off of his legs. He savored the momentary easing of his burden, even forcing himself to believe it was better than it really was. And then suddenly Ranger stood up on the plank and began to bark.

"Whose there Ranger? Is somebody comin'?"

Ranger left the plank just out of Phil's view and began barking louder and more excitedly. Phil recognized that bark. It was Ranger's somebody is in my yard warning. It was a typical farm dog greeting. Then came the voice, "Hey fella. What's got you so upset?"

Instantly, Phil's heart was hit by a surge of adrenaline that caused it to hammer. He began to shout with all that he had. "Help. Help me. I'm in the well. Help me."

Hearing Phil, Ranger settled down to an occasional bark but the stranger went silent. For a moment Phil strained to hear, thinking that maybe he wanted so badly for someone to come that he'd been hearing things. But he knew otherwise, he was certain of it. And so he yelled again, "Help me. For God's sake help me. I'm in the well."

Within seconds Ranger appeared at the edge of the opening above. He looked down to where he knew Phil was at and then he looked away and barked. Then came the voice again, evil and mocking in its tone, "Okay boy. You guard that well now. You guard it real good." Phil was about to shout to the stranger again when it came; laughter. Phil was taken aback. It sounded cold and wicked but who else did he have to appeal to. "Please, help me. Please, I'm begging you. I can't last much longer down here." But there was no response, nothing but the suffocating quiet of the well. Phil was beset with anger that soon metamorphosed into abject fear. He began to cry and did so for a good while.

The sun had gone down, he supposed, several hours ago. Phil imagined the darkness at the bottom of the well to be like somebody stuffing your eye sockets full of axel grease. He couldn't see a thing, at least looking straight ahead he couldn't, but if he leaned back and looked directly up he could see sandwiched in between the plank and the windlass, three stars. One of them was brighter than the others. In a strange way being able to see the stars gave him hope. They were his nexus to freedom.

It was a little past midnight when the urge to urinate came over him. Since being in the well he'd relieved himself twice. It bothered him, peeing in the same water he was standing in. *Just like some old cow standing in the crik doing her business while she takes a drink*, he said to himself. But the urine brought some momentary warmth to his crotch and upper thighs and the hard fact of the matter was, he had no choice. He knew too there would come a time, just like the cow in the creek, that he'd have to drink the well water.

In late June the days were long and the nights short. Phil could see that it was getting lighter to either side of the plank up above. He called out, "Hey Ranger dog. Are you up there?"

Ranger responded with two short barks. It brought a smile to Phil's face. "Yer ah good dog, Ranger, ah really good dog. When I git outta here we're both gonna have us some breakfast. I'll bet yer hungry."

Ranger barked again as if he had actually understood what Phil had said and then he got up and trotted off. Unlike Martha or the stranger, Phil was confident that Ranger would be back. Still, he had spent the night wondering what had happened to Martha. He had played in his mind all of the possible scenarios that could account for why she had not come back and none of them were good. He was fearful that she'd come to no good end. The stranger, on the other hand, caused instant rage within him. Even now the rage had not played itself out. Phil said aloud, "That sonovabitch ever crosses my path again I'm gonna beat his ass like a cheap drum." And then he took a deep breath and slowly exhaled so as to calm himself, but it was not an easy thing to do as the stranger's laughter seemed to be permanently stuck in his mind.

The opening of the well showed it to be getting real light outside the hole. Phil lit a match and pulled his pocket watch out by the leather lanyard attached to it and one of his Levis' belt loops. It was half past seven. A shiver of fear shot through him. *Most farmers have started their day by now,* he said to himself. And then his mind replayed yesterday when Jack didn't come and instantly his efforts to calm himself were negated. But then, suddenly, he could hear Ranger barking at the edge of the hole. It was that overly excited what are you doing in my yard bark. Jack began to yell as loud as he could, "Help me. Help me. I'm in the well. Help me. Don't leave.

Please help me." And then Ranger settled himself considerably like something had changed. Phil thought he heard a human voice. He paused and strained to hear when the light above was mostly blocked.

"Phil, is that you down there?"

Absolute relief swept over Phil. "Yeah, it's me, Jack. I'm damned glad ta see ya. I been stuck down here for a day and a night. Please, git me out, Jack. I can't take this any longer."

"Sure thing, Phil. Just gimme a minute ta git yer climbin' rope tied off here."

"I can't tell ya how damned glad I am ta see ya, Jack. I thought I was done for."

"Well where's Martha?"

A sudden sick feeling hit Phil. "I don't know. Somethin's happened to her."

"All right, watch yerself. I'm gonna toss the rope down."

And then, in the next instant, the excess of the knotted rope smacked Phil in the head but he didn't care. He grabbed for it like a starving man would food and immediately tried to climb up it but right away found that his legs were so cold and stiff and fatigued that they just wouldn't respond. Instantly his happiness turned to fear. He'd always climbed it when it had been him and Martha but things were different now. "My legs ain't workin' right, Jack. Yer gonna have to winch me up."

"Well then, tell me when to start"

Phil wrapped the rope around his upper torso beneath his arms and tied it in front of him. He was about to holler at Jack when he remembered the shovel and lantern. It was tempting to just leave them to rust away in the water as he'd decided long before now that if he got out of the well he was never coming back down it or any other well ever again. "Shit," he hissed. "Can't leave them down here." In the darkness the shovel was easy to find as he'd been leaning on it when Jack had come; it was resting against the dirt wall in front of him. The lantern, on the other hand, was hanging off to his right. Like a blind man he began feeling along the wall, every cobble rock and the dirt interspaces between them until he came to the lantern. Carefully, he removed it and threaded his right arm through its wire loop handle so he could still grip the rope with his right hand and the shovel with his left. At last he was ready to go. "Bring me up, Jack."

"Okay, here we go."

Slowly the slack in the rope began to tighten and then Phil felt a sudden tug as his feet lifted off the bottom of the well. Tears came to his eyes. Euphoria enveloped him, but lurking in the recesses of his mind was extreme sadness. Martha was gone. The anguish of not knowing the why or where had been kept at bay by the prospect he was going to die in the well, but now those demons were free to assault him.

Jack took the shovel and lantern from Phil and set them on the ground. "Can ya pull yerself up on the plank?"

"I think so but walkin' ain't gonna happen just yet."

"Well hell, crawl on yer hands and knees."

It was a struggle for Phil to hoist himself up onto the plank, which was barely a foot wide. The effort left him a little out of breath, as well as being cold, exhausted and emotionally spent. For a moment he sat there slowly untying the rope and getting his wind back. It felt good to not only see the sun, but to feel its warmth and to know his chances of surviving the day were in his favor. Finally, he looked over at Jack to ask what he already feared, "Any sign ah Martha?"

Jack shook his head. "No, but I didn't go in the house. I knocked, there wasn't any answer." Jack paused, so as to not appear to be indifferent to Martha being gone and then came back with, "So, how in the hell did ya manage ta git yerself stuck in the well?"

Phil's voice was tired and unsteady. "Somebody came to the house. Martha went to see who it was and just never came back."

"She left ya without even the bucket rope?"

Phil got on his hands and knees and began to crawl off of the plank. When he reached solid ground Ranger greeted him with face licks, Phil paused, "Oh what a good dog you are. Yes, I missed you too." After absorbing a good amount of licks he kept on crawling, well away from the hole and then stopped. "Help me up, Jack. I need to go check the house. I can't feature what could have happened to Martha."

Jack, who was a good head taller and 20 pounds heavier, took hold of Phil's hands and pulled him effortlessly to his feet. "Are ya good?"

Phil was soaked from his waist down but his entire body felt chilled. He took a couple of tentative steps towards the house. He said without looking at Jack, "I git my blood flowin' again and I'll be alright."

And then Jack answered the question that between the two of them begged to be asked, "I'm damned sorry I didn't come yesterday. My boy, Orville, got his self throwed off that buckskin stud horse he was so all fired set on havin'. Had ta haul him ta town. Ole Doc Petrov put some corset affair around his ribs. Doc says they're cracked. That boy ain't gonna be worth ah pinch ah shit ta me an' I got meadow hay that's ready to cut."

It was, at that moment, difficult for Phil to offer Jack much sympathy as the awareness he had narrowly escaped dying and the fact Martha was missing and might be dead were paramount in his mind. Nonetheless, he knew that he would forever owe Jack. "That's a bad deal about Orville.

Maybe when I git things sorted out here and find Martha I can lend ya ah hand puttin' up yer hay."

"Oh that's alright. We'll git by. Besides, with this damned drought it ain't gonna be that much of a crop."

"No, you saved my bacon Jack. If you hadn't ah come over and fished me outta that damned hole I cudda ended up like one ah them waterlogged squirrels that falls in yer horse trough and can't git out. No sir, I owe ya my life."

Jack's brown eyes got watery for a few seconds as he drank in Phil's appreciation and then he moved on. Although he thought it was pointless, he said for Phil's benefit, "We better git on down to the house and see if Martha is inside. Ya never know, she could be there and just overcome by some peculiarity and she can't come to the door."

Phil began to hobble down the coulee towards him and Martha's shanty. He called out over his shoulder, "You know, I'll bet yer right. It'll probably be my turn now to haul someone into Doc Petrov. That old geezer is gonna be gittin' rich off the two ah us."

Jack played along. "We'll take my truck. We can make Martha up a good bed in the back for the ride to town."

"That'd be real swell, Jack. I'm sure she'll appreciate that."

And then the two of them went on the last little ways, mostly in silence save for some inane banter with Ranger who no doubt was hungry. But the silence and their delusion ended when Phil opened the shanty door and reality slapped him in the face. It took all of about two seconds to see Martha wasn't there. The room was cold, not so much in a temperature sense but rather it had a foreboding aura of emptiness and loneliness. The intensity of the feeling made it difficult for him to even imagine her ever having been there. She was gone.

"Maybe we should look around outside," said Jack as if he'd not yet let go of the fantasy that Martha was there somewhere.

A tear overflowed Phil's right eye and started down his cheek. "It ain't too likely she's there, Jack."

"Well, we could check the privy and the corral. Ya never know 'bout these things."

"Alright, I'll look in the privy."

"Why don't you feed Ranger and I'll go look. Won't take but a minute."

Phil nodded. "I'd appreciate that."

The two of them trailed outside. Phil dropped off at a wooden wagon with narrow rubber tires. There was a faded blue metal water tank on the wagon. It held 200 gallons and was close to being empty. Phil turned the valve to fill Ranger's water bowl and then set it on the ground next to the wagon. Ranger began noisily lapping the water up. A rough pine box about two feet wide and three feet long by a foot high was located near the water tank. The box had a lid on it to keep the ravens, magpies and skunks out of it as it contained dog food. Phil was in the process of filling Ranger's bowl when he saw Jack coming back from the privy, which was about forty yards south of the house. He paused and made eye contact. Jack did not break stride as he frowned and shook his head. Phil turned away and set Ranger's food on the ground. The sound of the stranger who had laughed at him when he was in the well grew louder in his mind. He'd wondered, fantasized that this man had forced himself on Martha at the house and then after a time came to the well to taunt him. But then he thought, *you'd think anybody that wicked wudda said something more to me, really git my goat cause he'd just had his way with my wife.* And then from the corner of his eye he saw Jack coming from the corral. He could see plain as day that he had Martha's yellow sun bonnet. Instantly, his heart tripped on itself before beginning to sprint. Phil started towards Jack. When he was within about ten feet of him he saw the blood and began to sob. His legs all of a sudden buckled like he'd been hit in the hamstrings with a two by four. Jack allowed him to go to his knees and then he dropped down on the ground next to Phil.

"Found this in the corral. I'm sorry, Phil."

Phil's hands trembled as he took the bonnet from Jack. There was a good amount of dried blood on the part of it that would have covered the back of Martha's head. For a moment he stared at the almost black stain, as he did his mind involuntarily supplied him with images of how Martha could have parted with so much blood. And then he began to cry even harder. He clutched the bonnet to his chest with both hands unable to impede in any way the intensity of his grief. Like a rusty hinge that was slow to close, his upper torso began to sink towards the ground.

Jack reached out and gently placed his hand on Phil's shoulder. "I'm real sorry, Phil."

Phil continued to sob for a time before it slackened to the point he could raise up and look at Jack. His eyes were red and bloodshot and his nose was running. He took a breath and said, "We're peaceable folks, Jack. We barely got a pot ta piss in. How could somebody be this evil and mean spirited?"

Jack pursed his lips slightly and shook his head. "I don't know, Phil. God didn't create no more savage animal than man. You'd ah thought he wudda just left out that part of ah man's brain that cooks up such deviltry."

"It ain't right."

"It ain't but maybe we're gittin' ahead of ourselves. Maybe Martha ain't dead."

Phil snorted and shook his head. "All the time I was in the well I kept tellin' myself she was ok, that things will be all right. I guess I needed to believe that then but I'm outta that damned hole now and things are what they are."

"Well, however it is ya need ta go see the sheriff."

Phil sighed. "I just wanted ah homestead. Something that me an' Martha could point to and say, this is ours. Some place where we could live out our days."

"And maybe you'll still have that, but right now we need to go see old Wiley Hargis and git him to workin' on this. Now git yerself up. I'll drive ya into town."

Phil thought to tell Jack that he could drive himself to town but the prospect of it being just him and Ranger now saddened him even more. He said, "I'd appreciate that."

CHAPTER TWO

It was about 15 miles into Baker. The road going there started out at Phil's as no more than two tracks through the grass and sage that had been worn down to bare dirt. They wound their way through coulees and over mesas that, at times, were peppered with patches of ponderosa pine and, in some places, juniper and pinyon pine trees. The grass and wildflowers had come on strong right after what little snow they'd received that winter had melted. It had been a pretty site that gave a dry farmer hope there would be good things to come. But, as folks were fond of saying, *that's all she wrote.* Mother Nature cut them off from any more moisture without a bit of compassion as to the consequences of doing so. And now the land looked as if it was slowly dying, its color just wasn't good. It was going to be real bad for farmers if they didn't get some rain pretty soon, but right now that didn't seem to matter to Phil.

When they got within a few miles of town the county had graveled the road so folks wouldn't get stuck if it ever did rain. It allowed Jack to pick up the pace to about 25 miles an hour in his old truck. It was a green 1925 Ford Model T that clanked and rattled and was a good indicator of how many big rocks and holes there were in the road. But couple the look of the land with the ride and their reason for going to town it was easy enough for each of them to go to a better place in their mind. All of a sudden, Jack emerged. "I sure as hell hope old Wiley is in his office and not out gallivantin' around somewhere."

Phil stared straight ahead for a moment like he hadn't heard Jack and then he made kind of a sour face and looked over at him. "Well, you know Wiley. Between you, me and the fence post I ain't got my hopes up too much that he'll find Martha."

"He might just up and fool ya." Jack's lips had no sooner stopped moving than he regretted not being more positive, but the remorse was short-lived as everybody knew how Wiley Hargis was.

Before the oil boom had come the town of Baker had been beholding to the Milwaukee railroad and the farmers and ranchers for its livelihood. Back then it had been comprised of a few hundred folks engaged in providing other people the things they needed in life so as to make it tolerable. Still, even with all the money the oil people had brought, Baker's population was only about a thousand.

Whether his mind was elsewhere or he was committed to the urgency of their mission, Jack failed to throttle his truck down as they crossed over the train tracks near the grain elevators on the north edge of town. Regardless, he accepted none of the blame for bouncing everybody off the seat. "Sonovabitch. You'd think the damned railroad could smooth that out to where a man isn't in danger ah bustin' an axle."

Phil's words were slow to come and reeked of disinterest. "You'd think so."

Jack glanced over at Phil and Ranger. He thought about slowing down but sensed it wouldn't matter. He sped on over the gravel and dirt of Baker's Main Street. People on either side of the street stopped on the board walkways and pointed. They appeared to be saying, *Look at that damned fool. He's going to kill somebody.* But Jack roared on past the cars and trucks parked parallel on the sides of the street, past the hotel, cafes and mercantile with their frilly canvas awnings that shaded his accusers from the hot sun, dodging dogs and pedestrians until he came to the side street where the Fallon County Sheriff's office was located and then he throttled the truck down. A big black four door sedan with a gold star on the door was parked in front of the court house, a two story red brick building. "Well, I'll be go to hell. Wiley is here."

Jack had barely gotten parked next to the sheriff's car when Phil reached down to the floorboard of the truck and picked up Martha's bloodstained bonnet. He made no effort to avoid the bloody part of it as Jack had when he brought it up from the corral. For a moment he stared down at the bonnet looking like he was about to cry but stopped short of it. And then he abruptly shifted his attention to Jack. "I 'ppreciate yer haulin' me ta town. Yer ah good neighbor, Jack."

Jack sighed, uncomfortable with the gratitude, and reached for the door handle. "Well, I reckon we better go scout up Wiley."

The courthouse was surrounded by grass that was mostly brown due to the drought and green leafy cottonwood trees that had fared better on account of their deep roots. Even in his sorrow Phil wondered as he, Ranger and Jack went up the cement sidewalk that bisected this struggling oasis, *why in the hell don't they water this?* There were two flagpoles that rose up out of the dying grass, one for the American flag and the other for the state of Montana. But the air was still and the flags hung limp and gathered like a coat from a peg on a wall. They'd just reached the top of the steps and the big wood frame and glass doors when suddenly the one directly in front of Phil opened and a slender woman with streaks of gray in her hair stepped out. It was by reflex that she smiled and said "Good Morning" and then almost in the same instant her eyes dropped away to Martha's bonnet. A look of fear came immediately to her face snuffing out the cordiality that had been there only seconds before. Phil was taken aback by the woman's reaction. It caused him to hesitate for a moment before stepping aside and allowing her to escape. It struck him as strange that something he coveted could be so horrific to her. But he said nothing and went inside descending the steps just inside the big doors to the basement of the courthouse and another door. It was made of dark oak with a frosted glass upper half. The lettering on the glass read, FALLON COUNTY SHERIFF'S OFFICE. The three of them went inside. Immediately, they were confronted by a belly high counter made of smooth pine that had been stained a blonde color. It extended across most of the front of the room. On the drab, salmon colored wall beyond the counter was a gun rack. It was the kind that held the guns in a horizontal position. There were two bolt action 30-06 Springfield rifles and a couple of Winchester pump action shotguns. To the right of the gun rack was a large wall calendar from the Baker Mercantile. It had a picture of some majestic snow-capped mountains and pine trees that had obviously been painted some place other than near Baker. Beneath this were three dark green metal filing cabinets that were three drawers high. In front of these were two wooden desks, each had a black telephone sitting on it. To their left was a door with a small barred window.

"Mornin' fellas."

Phil lowered his eyes to the desk where the voice had come from. A skinny man with sunken cheeks, dark eyes and salt and pepper hair cut short with a droopy moustache that was also graying was sitting at the desk nearest the door with the barred window. A clear, cut glass ash tray with a smoldering cigarette was sitting on the corner of the desk.

Phil went straight to it. "I got a problem, Sheriff. I believe somebody has abducted my wife." And then he held up the bonnet. "I'm fearful they've done her harm."

Wiley Hargis held his tongue while he studied the bonnet. Shortly, the awareness that he was looking at blood overtook his face causing it to become business like. Still silent, he took up the cigarette in a purposeful way and took a long deep drag before exhaling it in a roiling blue cloud. "I guess you better tell me yer name 'fore we go too far down this road."

"Phil Caldwell. Me and my wife Martha moved out here last year from Lincoln."

"Well Mr. Caldwell, are there any witnesses to all this?"

"If there was I'd tell ya who done it. Hell, I might even have rectified the situation on my own."

Wiley stood up from behind his desk and started towards the counter. He could have passed for a rancher in his blue denim shirt, Levis and black cowboy boots but the badge above his left shirt pocket and the Colt .38 that rode high on his right hip gave him away. He stopped straight across from Phil and rested his hands on the counter. "So where'd all this take place?"

"Out at my homestead."

"As I recall, yer breaking out some ground on Corn Creek."

"Trying to."

Wiley took another drag of his cigarette. He was still in the process of expelling the smoke from his lungs when he began talking. "So where were you when yer missus got abducted?"

"Down our well."

A surprised look came to Wiley's face and he cut Phil off. "Yer well?"

"Yes sir. We're digging a new well. I was down the hole when somebody came to the house. Martha went to see who it was and never came back."

"She didn't leave you with any means to get out?"

"Well no, she was just going to be gone a minute. But Sheriff, somebody came after Martha left and they wouldn't help me."

"They wouldn't?"

"No, they just laughed at me. I'm wonderin' if he ain't the one that took Martha."

Wiley sighed real deep and shook his head. "This is a strange damned deal." He paused and took another puff of his cigarette. "So how'd ya git out?"

Jack chimed in. "I got 'im out this mornin'."

"So when did this happen?"

"Yesterday mornin'," said Phil.

"Ho-lee shit. You were in that well a day and a night?"

"Yes sir, I was. Worst experience of my life."

Wiley's eyes fell away to the bloody bonnet that now lay on the counter. "Where'd ya find this?"

"In the corral," said Jack.

"Anything else? Any signs of a struggle? Other pieces ah clothing?"

"No, I don't recall it if there was."

"Maybe you should come out and look for yerself," said Phil with some edge in his voice.

"I suppose I ought to," said Wiley as he glanced down at his right hand and the cigarette he was holding. The ash had become so long it was flaccid and in danger of falling on the counter and then it did. "Dammit, the cleaning lady gits real upset with me when that happens."

Phil looked at the Sheriff's nicotine stained fingers. They looked dirty and had an orange-ish hue to them. From there his eyes just seemed to go on their own to the ash tray on Wiley's desk that was overflowing with cigarette butts. Right next to it was a cream colored glass coffee mug that had dark stains running down its sides. It was heavy and thick, the kind you could probably drive a nail with if need be. All together these visual images allowed the words in Phil's mind to escape. "Dammit Sheriff, you need ta git off yer bony ass and come have ah look out at my place. There might be something that me and Jack didn't pick up on. God only knows what's happened to my wife."

To his credit, the Sheriff checked his anger although his eyes hinted otherwise. For a moment he just stared at Phil letting the silence between them say what he hadn't. And then he said, his words dripping with indifference, "In a few minutes I got a meeting upstairs with some FBI boys. Maybe after that, if I got time, I'll ride on out to yer place and look around."

"I don't mean to be uppity, Sheriff," said Phil.

"But you are." Wiley looked at the cigarette in his right hand. It had burned itself down, almost to where it was touching his skin.

"Don't you think I got cause to be that way?"

The Sheriff turned away and began, almost meticulously, stubbing the cigarette out in the ash tray on his desk. "I'll be out to yer place at two o'clock."

Phil looked to his left and the clock on the wall. It had a brass pendulum with black Roman numerals and ornate black hands encased in dark wood with a glass front. It made a loud rhythmic ticking sound. He read the clock and did the math. "That's about five hours from now. Whoever did this could be long gone by then."

Wylie scoffed and shook his head. He looked hard into Phil's eyes. "Whoever took yer wife is already long gone or they're sittin' right under our noses. Either way, me keepin' my meetin' with these FBI fellas and gittin' somethin' ta eat 'fore I head yer way on account ah I git sick if I don't eat ain't gonna make an iota ah difference. What's done is done."

Jack turned towards the door and put his hand on Phil's shoulder. "It's probably best we just head on home and wait for the Sheriff."

Phil looked at Jack and then back at the Sheriff like he had something more to say, but the Sheriff beat him to it. "Go home. I'll be there. Two o'clock."

Phil nodded. "All right, Sheriff."

"I'd be obliged though if you'd leave that bonnet."

Phil handed the bloody garment over.

A frown, somewhat quizzical in nature came over the Sheriff's face.

"What is it?" asked Phil.

"I don't mean to be morbid or upset you but this is ah helluva lot ah blood."

Anger suddenly contorted Phil's face into a look of incredulity. "I know," he said in a loud voice. "Why in the hell do you think I'm proddin' ya like I am."

The Sheriff's eyes darted over to the clock on the wall and then settled back onto Phil. "What time yesterday was it that your wife was abducted?"

Phil grimaced and shook his head slightly. "Oh hell, I guess around nine o'clock. Not long after breakfast."

"You ask any of yer neighbors if they seen any cars comin' or goin' towards yer place about then?"

"No, we come straight here, but I can ask 'em if that'll help."

"It might give me a startin' point cuz right now I'm thinkin' this is a fairly cold trail."

Phil followed the Sheriff's eyes to the clock on the wall and then he turned to Jack. "Can we make a few stops on the way home. See if anybody saw anything unusual."

Jack nodded. "Sure."

"All right then," said Wiley in a hurried voice, "I'll se ya at two o'clock."

The big door had barely closed when Jack spoke up. "Well, did that go ta suit ya?"

Phil sighed and mumbled something indiscernible before starting down the steps in front of the courthouse. It wasn't until he reached the bottom step that he gave in to Jack's stare. "You know, I think the Sheriff is probably right."

Jack played dumb lest he say it too and be wrong. "About what?"

"Martha. She's dead and whoever done it is long gone. We're just pissin' in the wind."

"You don't know that to be true."

"It's what my gut tells me. You saw the blood on her bonnet. Nobody could survive that."

"You just don't know."

"That fella that laughed at me, he's evil. He wanted me to die. There ain't no doubt in my mind if Martha tangled with him, she's dead."

Jack felt as if he'd been checkmated. He went quiet for another half dozen paces before breaking his silence as they neared the truck. "Gotta git some gas and then we'll head home."

"I'd buy yer gas, Jack, but I ain't got any money. Least not with me I don't. When we git to my place though I can pay ya."

"Not for today you won't."

CHAPTER THREE

They had stopped at the Baker Mercantile and filled the truck with gas. Jack treated them to some jerky, donuts and a couple of bottles of sarsaparilla. Phil was finished with his before they reached the edge of town. For a time, he felt guilty for thinking badly of Wiley wanting to eat before their two o'clock meeting but after a while that feeling was replaced with his general dislike of the man. Moreover, he was tired. Physically and mentally, he was exhausted. He felt like he was caught up in something that he didn't deserve and couldn't escape. As a consequence of all this, they'd not gotten far out of town when it came naturally to him to retreat to his own thoughts. They'd analyzed the Sheriff's behavior frontwards and backwards, to no good end. Jack now drove the truck at a pace conducive to Phil just staring out the window and occasionally petting Ranger. The main road heading north from Baker was bounded by a good number of homesteader shacks and lesser roads, but as a person got further out these signs of civilization greatly declined. It was an area populated by those who had come late to try their hand at proving up on 320 acres of free government ground. Phil recalled how he'd had to convince Martha that it would be a good thing to follow these latecomers. The government brochure had made it sound like utopia. All a person had to do was build a permanent residence on the land within six months and, at the end of three years, have one-eighth of the land cultivated and it would be yours. The rules even allowed for the homesteader to be absent five months out of the year, which definitely made the prospect of having to endure a cold Montana winter in a drafty shack more tolerable. Phil smiled when he thought of this provision in the rules. *You can't leave if you ain't got the money.* And then as if to verify his feeling on the matter they drove by the residual of another dream gone bad. An abandoned shack with its door wide open stood a short distance from the road. Its roof was on the verge of caving in and its windows had been broken out. A solitary corral that had been mostly cannibalized for its wooden poles was nearby. Just beyond these the family privy was tilted to one side. A Montgomery Ward catalog lay in the weeds near it, the elements having turned its pages to something bordering on paper Mache. Phil couldn't help but wonder if one day soon he and Martha's place would look like this.

And then Jack rescued him from his nightmare. "You suppose we otta start with the Walters?"

It was still about four miles to Phil's place. The Walters, however, lived about a half mile up ahead and close to the road. "Well, I don't reckon we can cast our net too wide."

"All right then, we'll start our detective work there. Ain't much that gits by Walters' missus."

The Walters were in their late twenties but relative old timers in this country as they were just starting their fourth summer. They'd just been granted a patent on their 320 acres proving that it could be done and that the government and the railroad weren't scamming people.

Jack brought his truck to a stop in front of the Walters shanty, a 12' by 12' wooden box with a slightly pitched roof that had been tarpapered all around its tin stovepipe. It had the usual compliment of out buildings, a root cellar about 30 feet to the north of the shanty, a privy about a 100 feet behind the house, a small chicken coop to the south of the house with a corral near it and a barn. A black Model T truck with a short bed was parked near the barn. The dirt amongst all of the buildings was mostly bare and packed down from car and foot traffic.

Karl Walters was well over six feet tall. He had blonde hair, blue eyes and considered himself clean shaven, although he generally had three to four days growth of whiskers. He was wearing bib overalls, a brown cotton shirt and a black felt hat. From the open door of the barn, he hollered out, "Afternoon men."

Phil and Ranger were first out of the truck. "How are you, Karl?"

"Well, I'm still on the right side of the dirt so I guess I'm doin' alright."

Phil and Jack politely manufactured weak smiles as they closed the distance between them and Karl. "Well, I'm glad ta hear that," said Jack.

"So what brings you fellars my way?"

Jack went quiet and shifted his eyes to Phil. Karl followed along.

"I've had some trouble come my way, Karl. Somebody took Martha against her will."

"The hell you say."

"Yesterday morning. We were workin' on our well when somebody came. I was down the well so I got no idy who it was but Martha never came back."

"Well, I sure am sorry to hear that. I know Edith will be too. She really looks forward to those little get-togethers her and the school teacher and yer Martha have to talk about books." Karl paused and then he probed a little. "I suppose you got the Sheriff ah workin' on it. He got any ideas?"

Phil scoffed and shook his head. "He thinks she's dead and whoever done it is long gone."

"Dead." The word, that single word, had exited Karl's mouth like a bullet from a gun. "Well, what makes him think that?"

Phil's eyes had gotten watery. "Martha's bonnet was left behind. It had lots ah blood on it."

The look of shock that was already on Karl's face intensified as if it had been a fire that somebody had just thrown gas on to. It was clear, even beneath his scruffy blonde whiskers that the color had gone from his face and the conversation had become uncomfortable. At the moment, he was incapable of talking.

"I gotta ask ya," said Phil, "Did you or Edith see any strangers come by yesterday morning between say about nine and ten?"

Karl recovered his voice real quick. "No, I sure didn't."

"What about Edith? She mention anything?"

"No, I don't believe so. In fact, I'm purty certain she didn't."

"Is she around? Maybe we could jog her memory just in case she saw something and didn't tell you."

"Well she is, but she's been down in bed the past coupla days. She's got some kinda die-fungus that I don't want no part of. Been thinkin' I might haf ta take her to town and see the doctor."

Phil struggled to keep his feelings from showing. *Martha might be dead and his Edith is too damned sick to answer a question?* He said, trying his best to sound sincere, "Well, I sure am sorry to hear Edith is not feeling good. Tell her I hope she gits better real soon."

"I'll do that."

Phil turned to Jack. "I suppose we should git on down the road."

"Next stop 'll be Malloy's I reckon."

"They wasn't home yesterday," said Karl. "I saw 'em headed towards town early when I was eatin' breakfast and then they came back by yesterday evenin'. Saw 'em when I was comin' back from milkin'."

For a brief moment, Phil considered saying something borderline sarcastic about, *how it was his bad luck that Karl had the details of the Malloy's coming and goings but no strangers.* He said aloud, "Well, I guess we won't bother ourselves with stopping there." And then he turned in the direction of the truck.

"Be seein' ya, Karl," said Jack.

Karl raised his big meaty hands and cupped them like an extension to the brim of his hat so as to give his eyes additional shade from the hot sun. "Good luck to you boys."

They walked briskly towards the truck being careful to not look directly at the Walters' shanty. It wasn't until Jack had started the truck that he said, "Did ya see the curtains move?"

Phil scoffed. "Yeah, I guess maybe Edith is feeling a little better."

"You know normally that woman 'll talk yer ear off."

"Oh, I know. She can drone on worse 'n ah swarm ah flies on ah gut pile."

"You think she's dodging us?"

Phil sighed. "I don't know why she would."

Jack shook his head and went quiet for a moment before moving on. "So where's our next stop?"

Phil appeared to be thinking as he pulled a pack of cigarettes from his shirt pocket and shook one out. "I reckon the schoolmarm's place might be a good bet."

"Miss Maricelli?"

"Yeah."

"She's an odd one."

Phil lit his cigarette, drew on it deeply and then blew the smoke towards the windshield. "Why's that?"

"Well hell, she's got a good job and what does she do but sink her money in that government ground." Jack laughed. "Guess she's trying to go broke like the rest of us."

"I reckon she's rolling the dice just like everybody else. I took my tractor over to her place this spring and broke out 20 acres and planted it to wheat for her. She paid me the going rate and nothing more. She's savvy about things."

"As purty ah woman as she is I'm thinkin' there's some men around here that'd do all her farmin' if she'd grant 'em some special favors."

Phil's expression remained serious. "I took nothin' but three dollars an acre from that woman."

"I didn't mean to suggest-"

"I know."

Jack sighed and shifted his focus back to the road and accelerated the truck on down towards Miss Maricelli's.

School had been out for several weeks so it was a good bet that Catarina Maricelli was home. She lived about a half mile south of Phil's and while she couldn't see his house due to a brushy ridge that lay between them, she had a good view of the road that went there. Her place, that is her little box like shanty, was situated in a sagebrush covered basin where the soil was rich. However, much of the land she was hoping to prove up on was located on broken hills, some of which had rock outcroppings. Her 320 acres taken as a whole was not all that desirable, as about half of it was questionable for farming but it was near the main road, such as it was, and slightly less than five miles from the one room school where she taught. There had been those men who had thought she was naïve and foolish for staking this piece of ground until they learned she had found and developed a small spring surrounded by a patch of chokecherry bushes at the head of a shallow coulee. It didn't produce a lot of water but it was enough for her personal needs and it was within a quarter mile of her house.

The raspy sputtering of Jack's truck had alerted Miss Maricelli that she had company. She'd been pulling weeds in her garden to the south of her shanty but she now stood in the front yard waiting on her visitors. At last they arrived. "Good afternoon, gentlemen."

Jack had never had any dealings with Miss Maricelli so he smiled and nodded, deferring to Phil who actually knew her. "Afternoon, Ma'am."

Catarina appeared to be in her mid-thirties and pretty. She was of average height but well- proportioned with long black hair and green eyes. Her attire was drab being comprised of a faded blue cotton skirt, a white blouse with arm length sleeves and a simple cream colored straw hat. She smiled politely, looking mostly at Phil. "What brings you fellows to my part of Eden?"

Phil removed his hat and took another step towards Miss Maricelli. He wasn't certain why he'd taken his hat off as he generally didn't in the presence of women. Maybe it was because she was educated or maybe it was her beauty, but he felt slightly intimidated by her. And then he said, in a sullen tone, "We've come on a grave matter."

Miss Maricelli's face became serious. "And what is that?"

"Somebody abducted my wife yesterday morning."

Shock and fear instantly radiated from Catarina's eyes. "Oh my goodness, I'm so sorry. I considered Martha a friend. She was such fun at our book club meetings."

"Thank you for yer concern, Ma'am, but can you tell me did you happen to see any motor cars come by here around nine or nine-thirty yesterday morning?"

Phil knew that in this area people didn't just happen to be driving by on their way to someplace else as the road ended a few miles beyond his shanty. Catarina's eyes lit up. "Yes, Mr. Caldwell, I did. It was black and had four doors. It appeared to be a newer car. I saw them drive by towards your homestead and about a half hour later, maybe less, they came back by."

"You didn't recognize who was driving?"

Catarina started to frown but caught herself. "No, not from this distance."

"How many people were in the car?" asked Jack.

Catarina glanced at Jack. "Just one, a man I think."

"Yer not certain?" asked Phil.

Catarina hesitated as if she was reviewing in her mind's eye the image of the strange car and then she said emphatically, "There was just one man."

"What'd he look like?"

"He had dark colored clothes and a black hat." Catarina paused and then added as if to defend herself, "The car was moving at a good pace, too fast for the road conditions I thought, but as I said, it was a long ways off."

Phil went silent for a moment and then he took a deep breath and exhaled it noisily. "I suppose if Martha had been in that car and she was able, or allowed to I guess, she wudda been sittin' up."

And then the awkwardness of what they all believed to be the obvious that dead people can't sit up took hold of Catarina in a way causing her to blurt out a half-truth as if it would somehow help matters, "You know, Mr. Caldwell, on second thought I believe I've seen that black car, or one like it, in town before. It was parked in front of those oil field people's office."

In the same tone as Catarina, Jack threw in, "Well yeah, you git some of those oil field boys from up ta Billings or down ta Denver and they spend half their time lost out here. One of 'em came by my place not too long ago sayin' he had the right to drill for oil on my land. Said he paid the government for the mineral rights. I told him to git the hell off my place. He said he'd be back with the Sheriff, so I guess we'll see."

Phil was about to dismiss the black car as an innocent coincidence when it came to him that the man who had refused to help him out of the well might have had nothing to do with Martha's disappearance and could have been some oil company guy pestering people to drill on their land. *Hell yeah, if I'm dead it'd probably be a lot easier for them folks to come right in and drill. But if the oil company guy was in the black car and he didn't take Martha then who did?* Phil looked at Miss Maricelli in a way so as to announce his intent. "Were there any other cars come by yesterday?"

Catarina appeared perplexed. "All day or just around nine to nine-thirty?"

Phil's heartbeat quickened. "Well, all day I guess. Maybe around mid-afternoon?"

"I heard an automobile go by very early. I wondered at the time, who in the world can that be at this time of day? The sun had not yet risen. And then as I've already said, there was the black car later in the morning."

"So you didn't actually see the car early on?"

"No, I was still in bed."

"Could you tell what direction it was headed?"

"It sounded like it was headed north, towards your place."

"If it was huntin' season it'd be easy enough to explain somebody being out at that time a day, but not now," said Jack. "It strikes me as being purty peculiar."

And then Phil knowingly plowed the same ground they'd already been over. "Are ya sure Ma'am that the black car was the only one to come and go once the sun came up?"

Catarina tried to hold back a sigh but could not. "I'm as sure as a person can be in recollecting events that at the time seemed of no consequence."

Phil nodded but said nothing allowing the sadness in his eyes to speak for him.

In deference to the silence that was quickly enveloping them, Jack tugged on the leather string that ran from a belt loop on his pants to his pocket and pulled out his watch. "Quarter till two, Phil. Do ya reckon we should move on?"

"I suppose but I ain't seen 'im go by here yet."

"You gentlemen are meeting someone?" asked Catarina.

"Meetin' the Sheriff at two o'clock," said Phil. And then he added sarcastically, "For whatever good that'll do."

"You don't have confidence in Sheriff Hargis?"

Phil could see that Catarina was serious and responded in kind. "Do you?"

"He seems to turn a blind eye to the moonshiners, but that's of no consequence to me. I'm not part of the temperance crowd. I'm just a single woman living alone in a remote area and I feel safe."

"Well, that's good Miss Maricelli. No one likes being afraid."

"No, I suppose not."

And then the Sheriff's car came into view on the far side of the basin about a mile from Miss Maricelli's place. A dust cloud roiled up behind it. Jack verbalized what they all were looking at. "Yonder comes the Sheriff."

Phil looked at Catarina and nodded. "Thank you for your help, Ma'am."

"You're most welcome. I hope you find your wife safe and sound."

Phil turned away and hollered for Ranger who had been playing with Miss Maricelli's dog over near the chicken coop. "C'mon Ranger. You've worried them chickens long enough. We've got ta go." Ranger came running, his tongue lolling happily out the side of his mouth. He jumped in the cab of the truck and took his place on the seat between Jack and Phil.

Catarina waved as Jack maneuvered the truck out of her yard. Phil waved back with a lack of enthusiasm that befitted their purpose for being there and for a moment their eyes met causing his thoughts to go elsewhere. In that instant he felt shame, and then the truck picked up speed and she was out of sight and he was back to reality.

As it worked out they followed the Sheriff's dust cloud to Phil's place. He was standing beside his big car with the gold star on the door when they pulled in. Jack's truck had barely come to a stop when the Sheriff hollered out in a tone like they were all friends. "I thought that might be you boys ah eatin' my dust."

Phil and Jack and Ranger got out of the truck. Before they could say anything the Sheriff came again. "Your neighbors see anything?"

"The schoolmarm saw a black car around nine headed north towards my place and then a little while later come back by," said Phil in a tone that bordered on exasperation.

"Said she heard another car go by her place ah little before daylight but she never saw that one ever come back by."

The Sheriff took a drag off of his cigarette and blew the smoke out before him in a thoughtful manner. "Nobody else saw anything?"

"Not that we talked to they didn't."

"She say what color the license plate on that black car was?"

"No, but she thought it might belong to one of those oil people."

Sheriff Hargis nodded. "I'll talk to those boys. Need ta talk to 'em anyway. Been gittin' some complaints that they've gotten a little heavy-handed about drillin' on folks' land."

Jack seized the moment. "Well, I hope you set 'em straight Sheriff. One ah them sons-ah-bitches came by my place awhile back and tells me he's got the right to drill for oil on my land."

"He probably does."

"Not in the middle of my wheat field he don't."

"Well, they've got these college boys that's been schooled in what you call geology and if they say the well needs to be in the middle of yer wheat field then I reckon you'll play hell convincin' 'em otherwise." The Sheriff paused and drew down on his cigarette squinting his right eye as if he needed to concentrate on sucking the smoke into his lungs. And then as the smoke began to tumble from his mouth he went on. "They gotta pay ya somethin' for damages – lost production they call it."

"I'll damn sure give 'em ah bill. Why, I won't be able to grow anything on that land as long as that well is there. Hell, that could be 30 - 40 years."

Finally, Phil jumped in running his words through a vat of sarcasm. "You boys reckon we could get back ta figuring out what happened ta Martha?"

Jack immediately showed some signs of being embarrassed but the Sheriff seemed un-phased. He came back. "Show me where it was you found Martha's bonnet."

"It was over there," said Jack nodding towards the corral.

The Sheriff and Phil fell in behind Jack as they trailed over to the corral. They went through the open gate and stopped at about the center of the enclosure. "As I recall, it was right here," said Jack pointing down at the ground.

Sheriff Hargis took another drag of his cigarette as he stared down at the spot Jack was pointing to. He exhaled the smoke. A slight breeze caught it and carried it away. Not too far off a Meadowlark punctuated the silence that had come with the Sheriff's fixation on the ground where the bloody bonnet had been. Still, he continued to stand where he was but shifting his eyes from the bare ground before him to the rest of the corral. The Meadowlark sang twice more before the Sheriff purged his mind. "Somethin' ain't right here."

"Whaddaya mean, Sheriff?" asked Phil.

"It don't make sense yer wife's bonnet being here. It had lots ah blood on it. In my country boy opinion it wudda stained the dirt as I'm thinkin' she wudda been down on the ground – bleedin'. But I don't' see that here and I don't see any signs of a struggle or drag marks."

"I guess we was thinkin' the wind blew it down here."

Sheriff Hargis looked over at the corral fence. Weeds, about two feet tall had grown up next to it. They made a good windbreak. He looked back at Phil. "I don't think that's likely."

"So what are you thinking?"

"Well, if you boys didn't find any blood or signs of a fight in the house or anywhere else that pretty much means, at least to me it does, that she was struck inside the car and our boy threw the bonnet in the corral hopin' it wouldn't be noticed for a while."

Phil wanted to believe that Martha was still alive but all this talk about blood and fighting and the Sheriff's tone, almost like it was a given that she was dead, made it difficult for him to believe she wasn't. It was a struggle to keep from tearing up. Phil drew a breath to steady his voice. "Do ya suppose we should organize a search party?"

The Sheriff sighed like Phil's request had caused him pain or at a minimum annoyance. "I suppose we could but where would you start?"

"Here, I guess," said Phil like it was the obvious.

"Well, let's ponder this situation, Mr. Caldwell. The schoolmarm says there was two cars come this way but only one came back, at least that she saw. And you say that Martha left to see who had come to the house and then later this stranger comes to the well and laughs at you. Now it could be that the man who laughed at you and Martha's abductor are one in the same or it may be there were two different men. The first abducts Martha and skedaddles right pronto. I'm thinkin he's not gonna want ta stop and dispose of a body anywhere near here. He's just gonna get on down the road as far away as he can git. But, it may be the laughing man saw our abductor. There's our witness. Why hell, he cudda met 'im drivin' in here."

"So you think you can track this fella down?"

"Well sir, if he is one ah them oil company boys I believe I can."

Phil was reluctant to backtrack on his earlier criticism of Wiley Hargis to Jack, but he was beginning to have more respect for his abilities. "I guess you'll let me know what you find out."

"I will just as soon as I know something."

CHAPTER FOUR

The dust from the Sheriff's car was still hanging in the air over the road leading away from Phil's place when it became apparent to him that he would soon be alone with his grief. From the time he'd accepted the fact that Martha was in real trouble and probably wasn't coming back he'd started thinking of her as if she was a memory. They were fleeting recollections, a particular time that she had laughed at something he'd said, her squeamishness at fishing, her voice saying nothing special but she was alive. And all the times they'd made love and the intense emotion that came with it and how he thought it would be impossible to duplicate that with anyone else. It was as if her being gone, permanently gone, had stripped him of the will to live. The sadness he felt gripped him as if he were in a strait jacket and it wasn't even dark yet. He asked himself, *Why would God do such a thing to a man?*

"Maybe you should spend the night over at my place," offered Jack. "Ruth Ann 'll cook us up a steak and taters for supper. Got some cherry pie too." And then he paused and smiled in a mischievous way. "I can probably scare up a little John Barleycorn too."

His fear of being alone tonight trumped any social etiquette whereby he would protest that he *didn't want to impose* and then wait for Jack to insist. Emboldened as he was, Phil came back quickly, "I'd appreciate that."

Mild surprise registered in Jack's eyes before he broke into a grin. "All right then. Let's head over to my place."

"We're purty early for supper. Ruth Ann will skin you alive, maybe both of us if we come waltzin' into her kitchen now."

Jack looked away and then back at Phil. His expression was serious. "We're gonna make a stop on the way. Got somethin' I wanna show ya."

Phil sensed that Jack was hesitant to share with him what it was that he'd just said he would. He figured there was only one reason why he would do such a thing. "Has this got something to do with Martha being taken?"

Jack had begun walking back to his truck. "I'll let you decide."

It was about a mile from Phil's to a deep coulee that intersected the main road. Nature had favored this drainage, which ran off to the east towards North Dakota for a good ways, with a modest stand of ponderosa pine trees. Few people knew how far it went, or the faint two-track going up the bottom of it, as there was a fence and locked gate about two hundred yards from where it began at the main road. Jack turned onto the tracks going up through the trees. It was cool and shady and soothing. Pine squirrels and Steller's jays were chattering overhead, announcing to all that something had invaded their home. They'd not gone far when Phil saw off to his right the little grassy area beneath the trees where he and Martha had come for a picnic. That'd been some time ago, not long after they'd gotten to their homestead and before she had soured on the whole idea. For a moment, he could see her in the clearing, pretty and happy, even laughing. And then the truck was past it and in his mind's eye the image of her flickered like a candle struggling against a gentle breeze before suddenly being gone.

Still in the trees, the road curved slightly and there it was jolting you out of whatever comfort you may have derived over the past two hundred yards, a red pipe gate with a sign, KEEP OUT –PRIVATE PROPERTY – OROSCO LAND & CATTLE COMPANY. Jack stopped the truck close to the gate and turned the motor off. A red breasted nuthatch sounded its shrill call letting everyone know the intruders had arrived.

"I think I know why we're here," said Phil. "But, nobody goes through Orosco's land. I've heard stories of him or his hands pulling guns on people they've caught hunting on his land."

"Well, if ya know the right people he'll let ya through."

"Right people?"

"I can guarantee ya that Orosco hasn't gotten all that he has from sellin' cattle."

An uneasy feeling came over Phil like he was sitting next to someone that he really didn't know. In a way he wished that he'd not accepted Jack's invitation, but it was too late for regret. "So, how does he make his money?"

"John Barleycorn."

"He's a moonshiner?"

Jack turned in his seat behind the wheel of the truck and looked Phil hard in the eyes. His tone was threatening. "You can't say a word, not to nobody. It wouldn't be healthy for either one of us."

"Alright Jack, I know when to keep my mouth shut."

"Maybe I shouldn't ah told ya but when the schoolmarm told us about that car coming by her place before sunup and then not ever seeing it come back, my mind went straight to here. It's how I'd git outta this country without paradin' back by every homestead between here and Baker."

"Makes sense to me but Pete Orosco ain't gonna let just anybody go through his land."

"I know and that's what scares me about this whole deal cuz he knows some bad people."

Phil became uneasy, almost fearful of Jack but he pressed on. "How is it you know these things?"

Regret had spread over Jack's face. It was the kind a man might have if he'd walked out onto a frozen pond and now the ice was cracking beneath him. "It's ah good while 'fore supper. Why don't we git out and have a smoke?"

Phil allowed Jack the dodge and got out of the truck. He followed him to a big downed tree a short distance away and sat down next to him. "Wanna Lucky?" he said shaking a cigarette part way out of the pack in his outstretched hand.

Jack took the cigarette and waited until Phil had lit a match before leaning close to the flame. He pursed his lips several times, kind of like a fish feeding and the cigarette came to life. He nodded. "Generally I roll my own but this ain't bad for a store bought."

Phil leaned forward, resting his elbows on his knees. He took a drag of his cigarette and spewed the smoke out over the stunted grass. He said, like he had lost interest in what they'd been talking about in the truck. "It's dry as hell here. We need to be careful with these smokes."

For a moment Jack said nothing and then with the cigarette clutched between the first two fingers of his right hand he pointed to a spot in the grass about ten feet away. "We ain't the only ones that needs ta be careful with their smokes."

"How's that?"

"Them butts over there in the grass. Somebody else has been sittin' here or in their car, maybe for a good while."

Phil probed the mostly yellow grass with his eyes until he picked up the white butts. There were about a half dozen that he could see. "They look to be pretty fresh."

Jack stood up from the log and started towards the butts. "Yeah, like around daybreak yesterday till about nine o'clock."

Phil got to his feet and followed after Jack. It was all coming into focus now, like somebody had sketched it out for him. They were close to the locked gate. A pullout, where people turned around, paralleled the fence attached to the gate. "These car tracks are fresh."

Jack looked over at the tracks and back to the butts. "He probably sat in his car smokin' 'til he worked up the nerve ta go over to yer place."

Phil had little doubt that Jack was probably right as to how things had played out. Still, none of it made sense to him. "I don't see how a man could be so purposeful in driving to almost the end of the road to take my Martha."

"Well, she was a pretty woman. Men will sometimes do some vile things for a good looking woman."

"I won't dispute that but Miss Maricelli is a purty woman too and she doesn't have any man to protect her."

"I don't know, Phil. Maybe it's just yer bad luck."

"But to come all the way out here?"

"My guess is one ah them oil field boys saw Martha at some point and got a fixation on her that couldn't be satisfied until he got hold of her. Some ah them boys are rough characters."

Phil thought for a moment about what Jack had just said and then he came back. "Well, you seem to know Orosco pretty well. Would he have any associates like that?"

Jack frowned and sighed. "Appears there's no gittin' around me steppin' off in this bog hole." He paused and then spit it out with some degree of agitation. "Hell yes, he knows people like that and maybe worse. I'll tell ya what, all this prohibition crap has brought out the evil in ah lotta men and Pete Orosco is one of 'em."

It was like Jack's fervor was contagious as Phil came back at him, just short of shouting. "So how in the hell is it you know so much about a guy who lives out here in the middle of thousands of acres of land that no one else can git to?"

Anger danced in Jack's eyes. "I work for him, that's why."

"You work for him? Doing what?"

"Runnin' shine."

"Moonshine?"

Jack sighed and nodded, his demeanor having suddenly turned to shame. "It ain't nothin' I'm proud of but I got a wife and two little ones to feed. How else am I gonna do that if it never rains and the damned grasshoppers eat what little crop I do grow? You know how it is out here so tell me, how am I gonna do that, Phil?"

Phil shrugged his shoulders slightly and shook his head. "I don't know Jack but the risk -"

"Risk? I'll tell ya where the risk is at. It's not doin' anything to keep yer wife and kids from goin' hungry and not having a roof over their heads. There's yer risk."

"But ya can't help 'em if yer sittin in jail."

Jack flashed a sardonic smile and scoffed. "It's been a long damned time since the sandman visited my bed. There ain't ah night goes by that I don't lay there wonderin' and worryin' that my next trip will be the one where the Feds sack me up. And after I've fretted over that for a while I switch to thinkin' about my wife and kids goin' hungry." He paused and laughed. "But the good thing about this time a year is the sun comes up real early and sets real late. Makes for short nights." And then Jack laughed some more.

Phil frowned in a pleading sort of way. "I worry too. I'm in hock to the bank for that tractor and plow I bought. They're gonna want a payment this fall and I ain't gonna have it."

"Well, I reckon then you can see how it is that I got mixed up with Orosco."

Phil nodded and took a puff of his cigarette. And then all of a sudden he bent down and picked up some wadded paper. He smoothed it to where he could read the writing on it. "Looks like our mystery man smokes Chesterfields."

"I suspect yer right. Looks like he sat here and smoked ever last one of his cigarettes, at least in that pack he did."

"Ya reckon he was just waitin' till he figured I'd be away from the house?"

"Well, it appears that is what he was doin'."

And then it became silent, save for a raven that had discovered them and was now cackling and circling overhead. The shade of the big pines felt good on a hot day like today. Phil could see how a man, even if his intentions were bad, could be drawn to this place not only to hide but to think about what he was about to do. It was like here, hidden from view, he was safe from the outside world. All of a sudden, it came to Phil. "We need ta search these woods."

Jack was caught off guard. "What?"

Phil paused to steady his self. Still, his eyes got watery. "If this fella killed Martha back at my house and then took off, here in these woods would be his first good chance to dump her body out."

For a moment Jack appeared to be thinking in a deliberate way. He took a puff of his cigarette and then exhaled the smoke purposely at some deer flies that had been pestering him. The effect on them was short-lived. He looked over at

Phil. "You know, I been thinkin' 'bout the Sheriff's take on what happened to Martha. I think maybe he's wrong about her being dead."

In that instant hope pushed the despair from Phil's eyes. "Why's that"

"Well, not ta be real ugly or cold about it but if this fella bashed Martha's head in at yer place why wouldn't he just leave her there? Why would he want ta take the chance of gittin' stopped with a dead person in his car?"

Phil's voice was dejected and tired. "Maybe it's like the Sheriff said. The guy kill– Martha died in the car. And then the guy tossed her bonnet in the corral and drove off figuring he needed to get away from my place before someone saw him there."

Jack sighed and shrugged his shoulders. "Maybe yer right. I don't know what to think, but if you wanna search these woods back down to the main road I'll help ya."

It gnawed at Phil's conscience that nobody had looked for Martha. A part of him acknowledged that his real motivation for looking now was to keep his guilt at bay and another part of him clung to the fantasy that she might be hurt and still alive. *Dammit, why did I listen to the Sheriff?*

"I'll tell you what," said Jack, "I'll cross over to the other side ah this two- track and work the woods back down to the main road and you can do the same on this side. That work for ya?"

"Yeah, reckon I'll stay near the two-track going down and swing out wider on the way back."

They searched, the two of them, slowly and methodically going through the forest in the bottom of the coulee. Neither wanted to be the one to find what they figured would be Martha's bloated and bloody body. But the Sheriff was right, at least for now he was, as Martha wasn't there.

CHAPTER FIVE

It was about three miles from the locked gate in the wooded coulee to Jack's place. They were about halfway there with neither of them having broached the subject of Pete Orosco when Phil, just out of the blue, came back to it. "Does Ruth Ann know yer runnin' shine?"

Jack continued looking straight ahead, his right hand resting loosely on the steering wheel. "I kept it from her for a little while but I ain't a good liar."

"Is she ok with it?"

"No, but fifty dollars a trip seems ta help her tolerate it."

"Damn, that's purty good wages for a day's work."

Jack scoffed and tossed his head back. "Orosco is the one makin' all the money. Hell, they'll take my truck if they was ta catch me."

"And throw you in jail and take some money outta yer pocket as well."

Jack glanced at Phil almost like he resented being told again what could happen to him. "If you had kids you'd probably risk yer neck too. If it was just me an' Ruth Ann and we was ta git put out of our house, such as it is, we'd make do. But kids, that makes it different."

Phil could see the worry on Jack's face as plain as if it was beads of sweat. He felt bad for him. "If I could Jack, I'd help ya, but hell my boat's leakin' just as bad as yers is."

Jack nodded his appreciation. Up ahead and off to the right on a yellow grass mesa was his shanty. He forced a smile. "Maybe we shouldn't stew over these money matters just now. Might ruin our supper."

Phil laughed politely. "Yer probably right."

"We'll have us a snort or two of the white mule. That'll put some lead in yer pencil."

Again, Phil laughed lest he stray from the carefree façade that Jack had just suggested. But then it came to him. *Hell, Martha's likely dead and I'm about to drink whiskey and eat a steak. What am I doing here? Martha's probably layin' dead in the brush somewhere. Ravens peckin' her eyes out and bugs crawlin' on her. And I'm about to drink whiskey and eat ah steak. What a sorry bastard you are, Phil Caldwell.*

Jack stopped the truck beside his shanty. He was out on the ground almost before the motor had sputtered its last. Two kids, Orville aged 14 and Jenny 11 came running. They were smaller versions of their parents. The boy had dark hair, brown eyes and was husky. His sister had red hair, green eyes and was slender. "Kids, you remember Mr. Caldwell."

Phil continued on around the front of the truck. Orville was quick to come to him with his hand outstretched. "It's good to see you again, sir."

Phil shook the boy's hand. It was a firm shake. "Good to see you, Orville."

"You stayin' for supper?"

"He is," said Jack.

"And how are you, Jenny?"

Jenny stood where she was. She said, barely above a whisper, "I'm doing fine, Mr. Caldwell. Thank you for asking."

And then Phil saw Ruth Ann emerge from the box like shanty and start towards the calamity his arrival had caused. Ranger and the Schneider's dog Heckles bounced along beside her barking occasionally and rearing up for a pet. Ruth Ann was thin and appeared tired, still she managed to temporarily overpower the beginnings of the worry lines in her face with a smile. "It's good to see you, Mr. Caldwell."

"And you as well, Ma'am."

And then suddenly her smile disappeared. There was instant sorrow in her eyes. "I'm terribly sorry to hear about Martha."

Phil was taken by surprise as he and Jack had not been there today.

"Paul Lewis was by with the mail. I guess somebody at the courthouse told him."

Phil had not given any thought to the fact he would likely be expected to regurgitate the images of what might have happened to Martha for all those offering their condolences. But at this moment, he couldn't do it. He thought to say, *Apparently, Wiley Hargis has wasted no time in sharing my business.* Painful seconds dragged on before he replied. "Oh, I thank you for yer concern."

Jack stepped close to Ruth Ann and put his arm around her shoulder. "I invited Phil to supper. He'll probably spend the night."

"Why, of course."

Phil could see the sincerity in her eyes. It gave him a good feeling.

"Orville," said Ruth Ann, "get a plate and a knife from the house and go cut Mr. Caldwell a nice steak."

"Okay Ma."

"And bring back a couple more spuds."

Orville raised his right hand to acknowledge that he'd heard his mother but kept going.

"I hate puttin' you out like this," said Phil.

"It's no trouble," replied Ruth Ann.

"It's been quite some time since I had a steak."

An uneasiness bordering on embarrassment came over Ruth Ann's face. Phil saw it causing him to follow suit.

Jack said flatly. "We eat steak probably once a week. Mr. Orosco was kind enough to give us a beef."

Mild shock came over Ruth Ann's face.

"There are some advantages to havin' Mr. Orosco for a neighbor," said Jack in a coy voice.

The unspoken communication between Jack and Ruth Ann was obvious but Phil did not allow his eyes to dwell upon it. He came back. "I reckon there is."

"C'mon over to the root cellar and I'll show you another."

Ruth Ann frowned. "Jack, supper is not long off."

"I know. We'll be along in time to wash up."

Ruth Ann held to her look of displeasure before turning away quickly enough to cause her long red ponytail to flip up. "Come along Jenny. You can help with supper."

Phil watched as mother and daughter marched back towards the house, their ankle length gingham dresses snagging on stems of sagebrush that had been broken off by Jack's truck having repeatedly parked there. Not wanting to be the cause of trouble, Phil said, "I'm alright if we don't go to the root cellar."

Jack shook his head. "Maybe you are but I ain't."

The root cellar was about 30 feet south of the house. It was discernable only by a slight mound of grass covered dirt over its roof and a trench about three feet wide with hard-packed dirt steps leading down to a heavy wooden door. A stout metal hasp about two inches wide with a whittled peg held the door shut, but not now as Orville was inside and the door was not latched. Jack and Phil stepped inside. Had it not been for the lantern hanging from the ceiling that Orville had lit, the room would have been dark as molasses. Two hind quarters of beef were suspended from a log beam overhead that was about eight inches in diameter. On the walls around the room were shelves filled with jars of fruit and vegetables and beneath these in the corner to their left was a potato bin. A small table about three feet by two feet sat in the middle of the room. It had a white glass plate on it. Orville turned away from the quarter he was cutting on and tossed a bloody piece of meat on the plate. "I hope you like yer steaks thick, Mr. Caldwell. I believe I've carved ya off one that will founder most men." And then he laughed.

Phil glanced at the steak. "That's a good lookin' piece of meat, Orville. I won't need ta eat for a week if I put that away."

Orville laughed again. "No sir, I don't believe you will." And then he picked up the plate and a couple of potatoes that he had put on the table and left, opening and closing the door as quick as possible so as to keep the coolness in.

The gas lantern sputtered and hissed as it struggled to light the room which was about 12 feet deep by 10 feet wide. "You've got it good here," said Phil. "It's easier for me to see now why you do business with Orosco."

"My family is my world."

"Do yer kids know what you do for Orosco?"

"Jenny doesn't but I sometimes think Orville sees through my lies."

"He's a good kid. I doubt that he'd hold it against you"

"I wish he didn't have to make that choice."

Phil nodded. "Maybe we'll git some rain and our crops will grow and you can quit Orosco."

Jack scoffed and pulled a mason quart jar off the shelf in front of him. He removed the brass lid and held the jar up in front of him. "To rain and to hell with Orosco." He then took a long drink and made a nasty face before handing the jar to Phil.

Phil repeated the toast and took a deep swig of the moonshine. It took his breath away and caused him to grimace. "Damn, that's some stout stuff."

"Probably a hundred twenty proof or so, I ain't sure. But I don't think it'll kill ya. I've seen Orosco's still. It's clean."

Phil laughed. "That's good ta know. It'd be a real slap in the face if a fella risked his money and freedom for a drink that killed him."

"Well, I'm particular about whose shine I drink. Been too many people end up dead or blind or somethin' else seriously wrong with 'em from drinkin' some fool's concoction that didn't care what went into it."

"They say a fella can test moonshine by puttin' a match to a little of it. If it burns blue flame it's ok but if it's yellow it's bad stuff and could cause ya ta go blind."

"Well we can lite some up if yer concerned but I been drinkin' it purty much since all this Prohibition nonsense became law and hell, that's been a good while and I'm still standin'."

"Oh no, I was just sayin' what I'd heard. I trust you wouldn't give me somethin' that was bad." Phil took another long sip of the clear liquid and extended the jar to Jack.

Jack took another drink. He was standing close to where the gas lantern was hanging causing his head to be silhouetted in the brilliant white light. For not yet being 40 he had more than his share of wrinkles. Droplets of moonshine glistened in his unruly black moustache before he sensed they were there and wiped them away. The shine was taking effect as his eyes had become glossy. He handed the jar back to Phil. "Ya know, I'm sure these temperance do gooder hussies would say that I've been overtaken by the evils of drink, but I'll tell ya what, after ah few snorts ah John Barleycorn all my worries don't seem ta matter as much."

Jack's words reverberated in Phil's mind as being fool hardy but he took the jar back and drank some more as he could still see Martha lying dead somewhere and come tomorrow it would be just him and Ranger. The thought of being without Martha scared him. When he really honed in on it, as he was now, it made him weak in the knees and feel like he could lose control of his bodily functions. He took another drink of the moonshine. Its burning and bitterness were not so much now. He needed badly to get away from the images in his mind. "I don't mean ta dig in ta yer business Jack, but do ya mind tellin' me where it is ya haul Orosco's shine to?"

In spite of the liquor, the relaxed nature of Jack's expression suddenly went away. It was like a door had suddenly been slammed in Phil's face. He retreated from his words real quick. "I'm sorry, Jack. I shudda known better."

Jack shook his head to the side and back in an exaggerated way before deliberately staring into Phil's face. He sighed deeply. "Some ah these boys play fer keeps. Orosco might be the least ah my worries if certain customers of his was to find out that I shared their business with an outsider."

Suddenly, it was as if a kaleidoscope was rotating in Phil's mind of all the bad things that had happened to him in the past two days. He just wanted to be a landowner, a farmer, and now here he was immersed in murder and bootlegging. "That's ok, Jack. It's probably a good thing I don't know."

"This business isn't for idle gossip, but if ya ever had an interest in hiring on with Orosco I might be justified in tellin' ya ah little more."

"Oh, I'd never wanna do that."

Jack smiled in a devilish way. "The wolf gits ah little closer to yer door and you might surprise yerself what you'll do ta keep 'im out."

And then suddenly the cellar door opened and there stood Orville in the shaft of natural light. "Pa, Ma says you and Mr. Caldwell need to come wash up cuz supper's just about ready."

"Alright Orville, we'll be along shortly."

"Ma said ta tell ya that if I come back without you and Mr. Caldwell that she'll be comin' with her broom to fetch the both of ya."

Jack laughed as he began screwing the lid on the jar. "Well alright then. I got no need ta git crosswise with the cook. We'll be right behind ya."

It was in that instant Phil reined in the opinion he'd begun to form of Jack's relationship with John Barleycorn.

CHAPTER SIX

It was about mid-morning of the third day since Phil had taken supper with the Schneider family. Jack was gone on an errand for Orosco and wasn't due back until tomorrow. The loneliness had been painful for Phil. No one, not a soul, had been around. It gave him pause, and not in a good way, as to what this said about him. He wondered, with the times being what they were, if people just had enough of their own misery and didn't want to share his. It was as if a pall of gloom had descended over he and Martha's little shanty and the 320 acres of government land that they'd come to make theirs. He took solace where he could get it. From the first night on, he encouraged Ranger to sleep on the bed – something Martha would never allow, but it was her absence that had created this demon of sadness. And so here he was on this hot, sunny morning, he and Ranger, walking towards the mail box out at the edge of the main road. *I'll git a pulse of what people are sayin'*, he thought. Off in the distance, he could see the mail truck's rooster tail. Gradually the black speck at the head of the dust cloud started to take shape until at last it veered towards Phil and the little black box atop the juniper post. It came to a sudden stop in front of them but the inertia of the powdery Montana dirt caused it to roll over the truck and Phil. Out of the haze come a voice.

"Mornin' Mr. Caldwell."

Phil squinted his eyes and held his breath. He had never been formally introduced to Paul Lewis but everybody knew the mailman. He had a face that didn't fit the rest of him. He was tall, skinny and had a bit of a hunch back. When he took his straw cowboy hat off, he was bald as a cue ball. His hands and arms were wrinkled and peppered with liver spots. But his face had somehow avoided father time. It was smooth, absent of wrinkles, almost cherubic looking. Phil swatted the air several times in front of him before saying, "Mornin'."

And then, as if to just get it over with, Lewis blurted out, "Sorry to hear about yer Missus."

Phil opened his eyes wide. At the end of Paul Lewis' outstretched arm was a copy of *The Saturday Evening Post* all rolled up but with the address label on the outside clearly marked, *Mrs. Phillip Caldwell – Rural Route – Baker, Montana..*

Phil nodded and took the magazine. It, and the books she bought in town, had been Martha's link to civilized life and sanity on those long winter nights when the wind and snow was swirling around their shack. He came back. "I suppose it's the talk ah the town."

"Not like you're probably thinkin'. Most people don't know much about what went on."

"Do you?"

Paul Lewis began to turn red. "Just what Mrs. Hicks at the court house told me. She types up all the Sheriff's reports."

"Well hell, you probably know more than I do. Hargis said he'd come see me when he knew anything. Said he was gonna track down this black mystery car."

"That oil field fella?

"You saw him?"

"He didn't tell you?"

"I wouldn't be askin' if he had."

"Well yeah, I told him sorta."

"Whaddaya mean, sorta?"

"Well, the sonavabitch was driving like he was going to a fire. He musta had that big ole Packard wide open takin' his share ah the road right outta the middle. I had ta take to the ditch down by the Walters' place."

Phil's senses suddenly screamed at him. "This happened down by Walters'?"

"Yeah, Edith was out standin' in her yard. She saw the whole thing."

"The hell you say."

Lewis snorted in a derisive way. "Well, you know Edith. She's ah substantial woman. Pretty hard to miss her."

A surge of adrenaline, the bad kind, suddenly coursed through Phil's body. Karl Walters had lied to him or at best Edith had lied to Karl. Phil kept his anger to himself but came back just to be sure he was justified in it, "And what time do ya reckon this occurred?"

"Like I told Wiley, as near as I can recall it was around three o'clock or so."

"So when did you report this to the Sheriff?"

"Well, it didn't do me any damage so I was thinkin' ah lettin' the whole thing pass but it just kept eatin' at me that this fella just plain didn't give a tinker's dam that he'd run me off the road, so I finally went and told Wiley about it yesterday."

"You said this fella was one ah them oil people?"

"Well, there ain't many folks around here that can afford a fancy car like this guy was drivin'."

All of a sudden, Phil's eyes shifted to the ridge just south of his shanty. It caused Paul Lewis to twist around in the seat of his truck and look that way. A paint horse with its rider was slowly working its way down the sage covered slope. "Ain't that the schoolmarm?"

Phil nodded. "Appears to be."

"She's ah fine lookin' woman. If I was 20 years younger I'd throw ah loop her way."

Well this 'll git tongues ah waggin', thought Phil but aloud, he said, "She's my neighbor. Her and Martha were friends."

Lewis grinned. "A fella could wear his eyes out lookin' at her so I guess I better git on down the road." And with that he stepped down on the floorboard starter button. The raspy sounding motor did not hesitate to start and within seconds Lewis had his Model A truck turned around and was about to leave when Phil abruptly ran over and stuck his head in the passenger window.

"Do you deliver mail to the Orosco ranch?"

Lewis looked puzzled. "Nope. They come to town once, sometimes twice a week and get their mail. Ain't many people go out there."

Phil did not allow Lewis to probe the question. He said, "Ok, thanks," and then stepped away from the truck.

Lewis held his bewildered look for a few seconds before turning away and starting the truck back down the road.

Phil quickened his pace. Miss Maricelli had not yet reached his house but it was clear to him she was likely going to wait there for him. She made him giddy. He tried to think it wasn't in a lustful way but he knew better and again he felt pulses of shame, just like the other day when he and Jack had been at her place. And then she changed course, guiding her horse straight at him. When she was about a hundred yards away and it was obvious that they were looking at one another, he waved. She waved back, not in a big, demonstrative way but rather a subtle flick of her right hand rising up barely above the pommel of her saddle and then dropping down. Moments later, her horse reached the two-track he was coming up. He could see her face framed beneath a large pale blue sun bonnet with its strings tied off beneath her chin. "Good morning, Miss Maricelli."

Her voice was deliberately somber. "Buongiorno, Mr. Caldwell. How are you today?"

"I'm gittin' by, Ma'am. Thank you for askin'."

"I know this must be a very difficult time for you."

Phil looked away for a moment and then he raised his eyes to her sitting there astride her horse. "I won't lie to ya, it's painful. Me and Martha been together most of our adult lives. Her being gone is kinda like havin' one of my arms amputated and then tryin' ta go on and do the things I always did. It ain't easy."

"I don't mean to downplay your anguish with a well-worn platitude but I believe it to be true, if one can suffer through it, that time heals all."

"You really believe that?"

An uncomfortable look came to her face, like she needed to defend herself.

"I'm sorry," said Phil. "I do appreciate yer concern."

She allowed a few seconds of silence between them to acknowledge his sincerity and then she smiled and moved on. "I am the bearer of gifts, Mr. Caldwell. If you'll look in my saddlebags you will find fresh baked bread and chokecherry jam and in the other oatmeal cookies and a quart jar of my squash soup, which I promise you, tastes better than it sounds." And then she laughed as if she were setting an example for him to follow.

Phil smiled in response to Miss Maricelli. It had come spontaneously, a fact that was not lost on his grieving conscience. He stepped towards her horse. "Is it alright if I take the stuff outta yer saddlebags now?"

"Please do. You can put it in this."

Phil looked up to a white pillowcase that she held above him. "Thank you."

"You may want to put the jars in first otherwise you'll mash your bread."

A laugh that originated in the cynical part of his brain nearly escaped. *Speaking of platitudes, does she not think I've got the sense to pour piss out of ah boot?*

Catarina went on. "The cookies are in a tin of their own so they could go in next."

Keeping his focus on the saddlebag in front of him, Phil gently shook his head and smiled yet again. *She is definitely a schoolmarm.* And then with his makeshift bag full he stepped to the front of the horse and hefted the bag slightly before him. "I sure do appreciate this, Ma'am."

"You are most welcome, Mr. Caldwell. Martha was my friend. You both are."

"Martha considered you a friend as well. She looked forward to the book club meetings."

"As did I. They always brightened my day."

Phil paused uncertain if he should say what had come to his mind.

"Is there something troubling you, Mr. Caldwell?"

"Lately, Martha seemed all worked up over this book that you've been reading."

"The Great Gatsby?"

"Yeah, that's it. She suddenly became dissatisfied with what we have."

Miss Maricelli became uneasy. "It was my impression that Martha has never liked being a homesteader."

"She told you that?"

Catarina hesitated to the point her words became unnecessary but said them anyway. "Well, yes she did." She paused. "But, I don't think she held it against you."

Phil laughed. "I know better, Ma 'am. But hells bells, did she want to spend her whole life mendin' other people's clothes and waitin' tables? That's what she had in Lincoln."

"I think it was the amenities, Mr. Caldwell. The conveniences that Lincoln offered. Electricity, a phone, running water and people to talk to. When Martha came to our little book club meetings it was like a ravenous person had suddenly found food."

"I knew she had that need to talk to folks on a regular basis, that's why I encouraged her to go to yer meetings. But as of late, this Gatsby book had her all worked up about what we didn't have in life. It was purty much like she didn't believe we'd ever have anything more than what we've got right now."

There was pity in Catarina's eyes. She sighed. "I don't know, Mr. Caldwell. The book is preoccupied with wealth and decadence. Perhaps it was a mistake for people in our circumstances to have read it. It was akin, I suppose, to allowing a starving person to smell a freshly cooked steak but deny them even one bite."

"It's just a book, Ma 'am. Standin' here in the hot sun on this dry dirt is real life."

The schoolmarm in Catarina caused her to shake her head. "Books are powerful, Mr. Caldwell."

Phil scoffed. "I reckon it doesn't matter now."

"Maybe things aren't as bad as they look."

Phil smiled. "More platitudes, Miss Maricelli."

"Hope, Mr. Caldwell. You should not abandon it so soon."

Phil looked up at Catarina. Her persona commanded respect. If anything, she was not afraid to be who she wanted to be. She was wearing a white blouse that was snug enough to show the fullness of her breasts and Levis with men's black cowboy boots. There were some, who were likely cut from the same bolt of cloth as the temperance do-gooders, that thought she was too brash to be the teacher of children, that she could be a bad influence. But the kids liked her and the men who had the power to fire her seemed to melt in her presence. She meant well. And then Phil said, "I guess we'll see but I'm not an optimist in this matter."

Catarina gathered her reins a little more firmly. "I suppose I should go."

Phil caught her eye. "I thank you Ma'am for the food. I truly appreciate it and yer words of encouragement."

Catarina smiled. "You are most welcome." And with that she reined her horse around and started back up the ridge knowing that Phil would be watching.

CHAPTER SEVEN

The morning had been sunny and hot. It wasn't until almost four o'clock that the buildup of clouds on the western horizon had begun. They were the big billowy, puffy kind that usually held rain. At the time, Phil's conversation with Miss Maricelli about hope had echoed in his mind. He'd said aloud to Ranger, *Now here's somethin' ta be hopeful about. We've had our dose of bad luck with Martha bein' taken away. Maybe now God is going to favor us with some good luck.* But it was a quarter till seven and dark enough outside to pass for ten o'clock. Phil was eating a bowl of the schoolmarm's squash soup along with a slice of her fresh bread and looking out the open door of his shanty when the first rumble of thunder sounded. Ranger, who had been lying in the doorway with his head resting on his front paws, retreated inside and lay down next to Phil's chair at the table. Phil reached down and petted his head. "It'll be alright, Ranger dog. That thunder can't git ya in here." But then God, or whoever was in charge of the turmoil in the clouds above, discharged a deafening bolt of lightning that struck a juniper tree not more than a hundred yards away. The tree exploded in flames, burning furiously. Phil could see it right out his front door. Ranger ran and crawled under the bed as a second and a third light-ning bolt cracked and lit up the inside of the tiny shack. Phil got up and went quickly out the front door to assess what was going on. To his left, blue gray smoke was rolling in a thick plume off of the lone juniper tree. To his right, the sage covered hill that Miss Maricelli had ridden down that morn-ing had fire on it. There was little Phil could do. Thunder and lightning were popping all around him. He looked up. The clouds were as black as any he'd ever seen. He shouted, "Please Lord, spare my grain." But God was not granting any favors today. Hail, the size of cat eye marbles, began to pelt the ground. Its intensity built rapidly. Phil ran back inside his shack. The noise was terrifying. It was like a thousand demons had descended upon the roof and were hammering away in an effort to get at him. Phil stood amidst this horren-dous cacophony knowing all too well what it meant for him. His mind flashed back to that morning and his conversation with Miss Maricelli. *What's to hope for now?*

The deluge of grief and destruction lasted no more than ten minutes but when it was over, the ground was white and it was cold. Phil stepped outside while Ranger, not trusting that it was safe to come out, stayed under the bed. A wisp of smoke rose up from the lone juniper while the fire on the hillside appeared to be out. But there was something differ-ent about the sagebrush, it was naked and skeletal. The hail had sent its demons with their tiny little fingers to strip all of the leaves from the plants. So, while they had not suc-ceeded in breaking through the roof of the shack they had excelled in killing the sagebrush. Phil shook his head and began walking toward the ridge north of his shanty and the mesa above it where his barley was growing. It was about a five minute walk slipping and sliding in the hail which was a good two to three inches deep. At last he topped the ridge and was at the edge of the mesa and the 40 acres he'd broken out and planted. In his mind he'd conjured up images of what his field would look like but they did not come close to the way it was as he could not totally let go of hope that it would be ok, until now. "Sonovabitch. Is there no justice in this life?" He kicked angrily at the white slush. He railed, "Lord, my plate was already full." Tears started to come to his eyes. He wanted to give them full rein to pour out onto his cheeks but then he caught himself and did not allow it, as if to defy whatever forces in nature that had done this to him. His grain, all of it, was lying on the ground beneath a white blanket. He walked a short distance into the field, stooping, probing here and there. Many of the seed heads had been stripped from the stems. His crop was a total loss. Phil stood with his hands on his hips and looked over the devastation. He laughed, his tone sarcastic and hateful. "Well, eat up all you little critters. Supper's on me."

The confines of Phil's cabin were even bleaker now. Not only was he haunted by Martha's absence but his reason for being there had just been destroyed. He headed towards the shelf where he had placed the pint jar of moonshine that Jack had given him. *There's days when a fella just needs ta take the edge off,* he'd said. Phil was grim faced and purposeful as he took the jar down and began unscrewing the brass lid. *This has got ta be one of those days.* As the jar neared his mouth the smell of the moonshine caused him to gag slightly. Still, he took a big drink swallowing three times. He gasped from the burning sensation. It came to him almost right away, another one of Miss Maricelli's platitudes that probably was true, *the cure is worse than the ailment.* He reckoned he would tell her, the next time he saw her, that he had thought of a platitude when he got drunk by himself. He smiled as he could already feel the moonshine at work on his insides.

In the morning the jar of moonshine was on the floor beside Phil's bed. It was nearly empty. Through the fog in his mind, he gradually became aware of Ranger barking and someone pounding on his door. He felt as if he was having a bad dream and he just couldn't wake up. Finally, the light in the room became brighter and the barking and the voice became louder as he was being jostled. He opened his eyes to an excruciating headache and Jack standing beside his bed. "Phil, it's time ta git up."

"Why?"

Jack sighed. "You ain't alone in this. I got wiped out too. Lots ah folks did."

Phil rolled over and sat up on the edge of the bed. He was still fully clothed.

Jack looked down at the Mason jar on the floor and laughed. "Looks like you and John Barleycorn might ah over done it a little."

All of a sudden the intense pain in Phil's head was over ridden by a wave of nausea that was not to be denied. He bolted for the open door and fell to his knees in the mud outside. And then he began to retch. Up came all of Miss Maricelli's squash soup, which had been very good yesterday, and some bread and cookies too. After a time, he came back inside and took a chair at the table with Jack.

"Ya feel better?"

Jack had set the Mason jar on the table. Phil looked at it as if it were an evil associate of the hail. "It's amazing to me that people actually pay good money for that stuff."

Jack's face became serious, even defensive. "It's got it's time and place."

Phil sensed he'd hit a nerve. "I suppose it does."

"Ya gotta drink it in moderation, otherwise it'll knock yer ass in ta the dirt."

"I guess it doesn't matter one way or another, Jack. I'm through here."

"There'll be better days ahead."

Phil laughed. "Another damned platitude."

"What?"

Phil gestured with his right hand as if to disregard what he'd said. He came back. "Come October 15th the bank's gonna want me to give 'em three hundred and fifty dollars. There ain't no way I'm gonna have it. They'll take my tractor and plow so, even if I could find the money for seed and fuel, I won't be able to plant next year. Hell, I won't even be able to afford a biscuit and ah bean for me and the Ranger dog."

Jack remained quiet for a moment, his expression suggesting that he had something to say but couldn't bring himself to it.

"I know what yer thinkin'," said Phil. "I've done the math plenty ah times. Fifty dollars ah trip."

"Well, it appears to me the wolf has knocked yer door down and invited himself inside."

Phil's expression became agitated. "And that's a fact I'm well aware of." He paused and allowed the anger in his voice to settle out. "It's the idea I could go ta jail that scares me."

Jack laughed, his voice filled with a false bravado. "Well hell, at least you'd have a bed and three square meals."

Phil scowled. "From what I hear they don't let you lay around readin' dime novels just waitin' for yer next meal. They'll have yer ass out doin' hard labor for the county or the state somewhere."

"Maybe so but what else ya gonna do?"

"Honest labor. How 'bout that?"

Jack scoffed. "You might find the labor part ah that fantasy but you'll play hell findin' a fair wage that a man can live on. So you go right on out there and see how that little strategy plays out at the bank this fall."

Phil put his left hand on the table to steady his self and stood up. "I need a cup of coffee."

Jack came back quickly in a friendly tone. "Sit yer ass down. I'll make it."

Phil dropped back on to his chair. "Are ya hungry?"

"No, I already ate."

"Well, I was just gonna say if ya was there's some of the schoolmarm's bread that was fresh baked yesterday over there on the counter wrapped in that blue hand towel. Some of her chokecherry preserves to go with it too."

Jack had momentarily forgotten that Phil was freshly widowed and was about to chide him about the pretty and buxom Miss Maricelli paying him a visit when he caught himself and laughed. "Let me get my pencil and notepad and I'll take yer order."

"No, I didn't mean –"

"Ya got any eggs to go with it?"

Phil smiled weakly. "As ah matter ah fact, I do."

It was both fortunate and surprising to Phil that he'd been able to keep down the toast and eggs and coffee that Jack fixed for him. He and Ranger had lain back down after Jack had left and were sound asleep when once again there was someone at the door. Through the window he could see the big gold star on the car door.

"Afternoon Sheriff."

"You don't look like you feel good."

It occurred to Phil that having a hangover would be an admission of guilt. "Yeah, ya wanna keep yer distance Sheriff. I contracted some kinda bug. Feel puny as hell."

Wiley's eyes darted to the table behind Phil and the Mason jar with the clear liquid that stood about an inch above its bottom or just high enough for a person to have a rip-roaring hangover. But he was not above allowing a man to grieve. He took a puff off of his cigarette. "I tracked that oil company fella down, or at least I think I did."

"How's that?"

"He says it wasn't him that came to yer place. He even denies running Paul Lewis off the road. Paul says it was this fella's car but he didn't get a good look at his face. So I'm kinda snookered."

"Well, what about Edith Walters?"

"Oh, you know about her too?"

"Yeah, there's somethin' not right with her and Karl's stories. Seems to me they see what they wanna see."

Wiley took another drag off of his cigarette. "Yeah, I sense a foul odor when I talk to those two. After I filled in a few of the blanks for Edith, her memory suddenly came back. Said she saw the whole thing with Lewis being run off the road but didn't think too much of it so she didn't mention it to Karl. I'm not sure what to make of it."

Phil suddenly changed course. "Well did you check inside this fella's car for blood? He might ah been the one that took Martha."

"I did. Couldn't find a thing. This fella says he doesn't know you or Martha."

Phil sighed. "I don't know that there's a law against leavin' a man to die in a well but, just the same, I'd like ta know who this guy is?"

"I can't tell you that."

"Why's that?

"Because there's no proof this fella was at yer place or ran Lewis off the road. The only thing he's guilty of is driving a black car near yer place at about the same time as Martha's disappearance and the man laughing at you when you asked him for help. This guy says he wasn't there. So, I don't need you tryin' ta improve his memory."

"Well Sheriff, I'd be willin' ta bet ya he's guilty on both counts. He might even have been the one who took Martha."

"That's for me to figure out."

Phil gave the Sheriff a disgusted look. "Well, so far I haven't seen much progress along those lines."

The Sheriff became angry. "Mr. Caldwell, I understand yer bein' upset about yer wife. Any man would be, but pissin' me off by insultin' me is not a wise thing ta do. I promise ya, it's not."

"I'm sorry Sheriff. A lot's happened to me these past few days. I guess it just got the better of me."

"I take it the hail wiped you out too."

Phil nodded, unable to look at the Sheriff. "I got nothin' left."

"Whaddaya aimin' ta do?"

"I don't know."

And then it was as if the Sheriff had been privy to Phil and Jack's conversation that morning. "I hate ta see this much misfortune come ta folks. Makes 'em do things they shouldn't."

"Sometimes people ain't got a choice."

Wiley Hargis smiled. "Oh, they always got a choice. It's just sometimes they don't make the right one."

The Sheriff's intuition caused Phil's insides to tie themselves in an even tighter knot. *It's like he already knows.*

The Sheriff turned and started back through the mud to his car. He shouted over his shoulder. "It's too bad all this moisture had to come down rock hard."

Phil scoffed. "Yeah it might have grown somethin' other than more misery for folks."

At first the rear wheels of the Sheriff's car just spun in place shooting chunks of mud out behind it. *Well shit, he's gonna expect me ta git behind him and push,* said Phil to himself. He sighed and started towards the car. Heavy globs of mud clung to each foot. *I'll be the envy of every pig around.* And then all of a sudden the car got traction and shot forward. The Sheriff waved a "thanks anyway" and gently accelerated the big automobile so as to keep his momentum. Phil stood in front of his shanty and watched the lawman get progressively farther away. He shook his head. *I'll probably never see that man out here again. I'm sorry Martha.*

CHAPTER EIGHT

From the locked gate the road continued on up the wooded coulee for about another mile and then climbed out of it and angled to the northeast across a mesa covered mostly by grass with a sprinkling of wildflowers and a few sporadic ponderosa pine trees. It was here that a good number of Hereford cows and the ghosts of buffalo were doing their best to convert the grass into manure.

"If I owned all of this I wouldn't risk it by makin' moonshine," said Phil.

Jack swerved slightly to miss a badger hole in the road. "I can't say that I would either but for some folks just makin' a livin' ain't enough."

"Yer sayin' Orosco's greedy?"

Jack grimaced and shook his head slightly. "It's more like his ego won't let him do anything less. I tend ta think he gits some satisfaction in outwitting the Revenuers. He doesn't like the government tellin' him that he can't have a drink if he wants."

"There's lots ah folks that feel that way."

"Well, more of 'em shudda showed up and voted then."

"I suppose so but it still seems ta be a slap in the face to common sense the government tryin' to stop people from drinkin' when there's so many of them that want to do it."

Jack laughed. "Well, it's probably good that they do otherwise we'd just be ah coupla hail busted farmers with no prospects for makin' ah livin'."

"We could still end up that way if we go ta jail."

Jack frowned. "It's too late for thinkin' like that. Tell me now if you don't want ta do this and I'll turn this truck around."

Phil regretted saying what he had. He'd told himself last night that he wouldn't mention jail anymore, after he'd taken stock one more time of the fact that he had a grand total of $33.47 to his name and owed the bank $1,214.79 of which $350 was due on November 1st. He came back. "I'm sorry, Jack. I don't mean ta be ah nervous Nellie."

"Well, ya gotta cut it out. You keep talkin' 'bout goin' ta jail and it'll come ta pass."

Phil felt like he was a child amongst men or good amongst evil or whatever it was, he didn't fit. He saw no way out. It was like he was back in the well again and his only hope of being rescued was through Pete Orosco. The truck had slowed and he could feel Jack's glare waiting for his response. He looked over and nodded. "Alright Jack, I won't talk about it anymore."

Jack sighed deeply. "You ain't the only one that thinks about that shit, ya know." And then he looked back to the road.

Phil kept quiet. They drove on for another five miles across land dissected with brush and tree choked coulees, an occasional trickle of a creek and grassy mesas and rocky buttes, all of it belonging to the Orosco Land & Cattle Company. The road had been steadily climbing across a mesa for the past half mile when all of a sudden it reached the edge, overlooking a valley which was carpeted by big ponderosa pine. A creek that looked like it could have fish in it was defined here and there by quaking aspen and willows. The water did not run in a straight line but meandered like it couldn't decide whether to go left or right. From high up on the mesa it looked like paradise to Phil. Situated on the far end of the valley was a huge log house with a covered front porch, a pine board barn and chicken coop, a large log bunkhouse and a shop. Near the barn was an extensive set of corrals. "I take it that's Orosco's place down there," said Phil.

Jack nodded as he started the truck down the dug-way road leading to the valley floor. "Nobody comes to Orosco's from this direction without being seen from the house."

Out of the blue, as they'd not talked about Martha that morning, Phil came back, "Stands ta reason then, somebody down there likely saw who it was that took Martha." That suspicion had been in his mind ever since they'd come onto Orosco's land but, until now, there'd not been the catalyst to bring it out.

There was a hint of annoyance in Jack's eyes. "Yer assumin' the guy came this way."

"Well, Wiley says there was no blood in that oil fella's car so there's got to have been somebody else that came to my house that day and, unless they sprouted wings and flew away, how else but through Orosco's place could they have gotten out."

"I don't know Phil, but I can tell ya it won't sit well with Orosco to bring up Martha's situation, at least not today it won't. Be kinda like yer accussin' him ah somethin'."

Phil's expression had become almost hateful. "I hear what yer sayin' but the trail ah Martha's abductor is gittin' colder every day. And Wiley, he just seems ta be kinda done with the whole affair. So what am I supposed ta do?"

Jack's voice took on an anxious, almost pleading tone. "Maybe on down the line you could ask Orosco about Martha but not today, ok?"

Phil sighed. "Alright, I'll save it for another time."

Jack said nothing but drove on, carefully guiding the truck around the first of the two switchbacks needed to allow the road to gradually descend from the high mesa. It could have been a pleasant ride as the steep slope's northerly exposure had allowed the ponderosa pine to flourish all the way to the top where it crested and broke off to the south and the grasslands. The smell of the woods and the chatter of the squirrels and birds on either side of the road would normally have been soothing to Phil but that wasn't the case today. His heart was beating much faster now than before his exchange of words with Jack. He sighed and said to himself, *What the hell am I doing here?*

And then the road reached the valley floor where it forked. Jack went to the left. They drove on through this shady paradise that had somehow escaped the axe until suddenly they were there in front of the big house. A man wearing a flat cap, white long sleeved shirt and brown pants held up by suspenders was standing near the barn. He had no doubt watched them come down from the mesa. They'd barely gotten out of the truck when he called out to them. "Mr. Orosco is over here."

Jack nodded and waved at the man before looking at Phil. He kept his voice low. "That's Luther Siegler. He distills all the shine. Supposedly, the recipes he uses have been in his family for years."

"Recipes?" said Phil in a surprised tone.

"There's more to it than what you think, that is if you want somethin' besides just rot-gut."

As they neared Siegler he looked straight at Phil. He was about fifty years old with considerable gray around the temples and in his moustache that used to be black. His green eyes as well as his voice reflected indifference. "This the fella that's gonna replace Hockmeister?"

"I guess we'll see," said Jack.

Siegler nodded towards the open door of the barn. "Mr. Orosco is inside."

Jack and Phil walked past Siegler who then fell in behind them. To either side of the little procession were empty stalls and at the very rear of the barn were two doors that partitioned off about a third of its overall length. From behind them Siegler shouted, "He's in the tack room."

Jack went to the door on the left, opened it and stepped inside. Phil and Siegler were close behind. At first Phil was a little taken aback as there was nothing but saddles, bridles and harnesses hanging from the walls. But then Jack went to the right side of the room and stepped on a five gallon bucket that was turned upside down on the floor between two saddles hanging from the wall. After getting his balance he lifted his right foot higher onto a ten penny nail that appeared to have been driven into the wall a little too low. As he stepped up he grabbed hold of another nail above his head. He then pulled himself up and placed his left foot onto another large nail that was holding a saddle whereupon he disappeared through an opening in the ceiling of the tack room or the floor of the barn's loft; however you chose to look at it.

"Gotta be ah damned monkey ta git up there," mumbled Phil.

"How's that?" asked Siegler knowing full well what Phil had said.

Phil sensed he was being baited. "Ah nuthin', just thinkin' back how it was ah good thing I climbed lots ah trees when I was a kid."

"Well let's see if ya learned anything."

Phil kept his back to Siegler and began climbing. As he neared the opening, Jack extended his hand down and pulled him up. Siegler, however, ignored the offer of help and climbed through the opening on his own, a fact that Phil questioned in his mind. *That fella is a real hard case.* The room was much bigger than he expected. It extended the full width of the barn, about 30 feet and was close to 20 feet deep. It was a crowded space. To the right were bags of cornmeal and sugar and cans of yeast. To the left was the still.

"So you're looking for work are ya?"

The voice had come from the shadows at the far end of the room. A good-sized man was kneeling beside a 50 gallon steel barrel that appeared to be resting on two parallel rows of bricks about a foot high. Beneath the barrel Phil could see a steady blue flame coming most likely from a kerosene burner. He was not quite certain if he was the one being spoken to when Siegler suddenly hissed at him. "Are you an idiot or just rude? Mr. Orosco is talking to you."

The room had no windows. Natural light was virtually non-existent save for the slivers coming through the slats of the spire on the roof which was intended to vent the barn's hayloft but served now as a means of escape for the fumes generated by the still. Nonetheless, it was necessary to burn two Coleman lanterns suspended from wires attached to a rafter overhead that were about ten feet apart. They were, to Phil's way of thinking, not efficiently placed as the room was still shadowy. And so he directed his voice at the crouching man in the poor light. "Yes sir, I reckon I am."

The crouching man stood and looked down into the barrel. "Luther, you suppose this mash is ready to cook it on down?"

Luther took several quick steps towards Orosco. "Yes sir, I believe we can. I'll start it just as soon as this other batch is done."

Orosco came out of the shadows and past Luther towards Phil and Jack. He said over his shoulder. "Hell, just add to it."

Siegler, knowing that Orosco would not see it, flashed a look of contempt at being told how to do his job. He then moved to the big brass cauldron with the copper tubing snaking out of it and unscrewed a heavy cap about three inches in diameter. Following this, he placed a metal funnel in the opening and took up a smaller bucket and began transferring fermented mash from the steel barrel into the cooking kettle where it would boil and the steam from that process would percolate up through the copper tubing, cooling and dripping out as condensate into either gallon jugs or quart jars.

Orosco stopped near one of the hissing lanterns. Its light illuminated his brown eyes that were accentuated by the prominent crow's feet at their corners. His skin, on both his face and hands, appeared leathery and aged more than his 57 years might require. A broad gray Stetson, dimpled three times into a peak, hid most of his salt and pepper hair. He looked straight at Phil in an undisguised haughty sort of way. "So yer another one ah those homesteaders that's gone belly up, huh?"

It right away flashed in Phil's mind. *What a sonovabitch.* Nonetheless, he came back. "I've fallen on hard times."

"Jack tells me you're trustworthy, are you?"

"I like ta think I am."

Orosco laughed. "I've always wondered how a criminal could consider himself trustworthy."

"Maybe you should ask yerself that question."

"Shit Phil, be respectful," blurted out Jack.

"I didn't come here ta be talked down to like some school boy. I need work. If there's none to be had maybe I should just go on about my business."

"Alright Mr. Caldwell, settle yourself down. I didn't mean to rile you, it's just, and I'll be frank with you, I don't care for what the homesteaders are doing to the range. This country was meant for cattle. But that's another matter."

"Jack told me you needed another man to haul shine."

"I do. One of my drivers had a little run in with the authorities over in Bismarck."

"Bismarck. I don't know if my old truck is up to a trip of that length."

Orosco glanced at Jack and frowned and then came back to Phil. He sighed. "Well then, we'll let your friend Mr. Schneider here service our Bismarck customers and you can take his run over to Miles City. It might be good to switch up things anyway. Keep the Revenuers on their toes."

From the corner of his eye Phil could see the irritation in Jack's face but he didn't dare appeal to Orosco for a different run. He was torn.

"Well Mr. Caldwell," said Orosco in a condescending tone, "will Miles City work for you?"

Phil regained his focus. He came back, sounding almost military like. "Yes sir, Miles City will be just fine."

"I suppose Jack told you, I pay $50 a trip and your gas. That work for you?"

"It will, I have bills to pay."

"Fine then, be back here tomorrow morning at eight o'clock. You'll go over and back during daylight hours.

Some of these fools draw attention to themselves by driving the roads in the middle of the night. You're gonna look like you've got legitimate business in town."

"Alright, eight o'clock. I'll be here."

Orosco turned to Jack. "You better plan on spendin' the night in Bismarck. It's a long ways over there and back."

Jack's uneasiness with his assignment was readily apparent. He came back quickly. "A room and meals will dent my wages. Any chance I can git something ta cover that."

Orosco laughed in a cold way. "You're lucky I buy your gas."

"I'm the one taking all the risk here."

Orosco snorted. "There's enough risk for the both of us."

"Well, I'm thinkin' Hockmeister might have ah different idy on that. From what I hear the Feds got him locked up in the Bismarck hoosgow. His wife tells me he's gonna be in there for six months and they took his truck and fined him a hundred dollars ta boot. It appears ta me the risk has come home ta roost for Hockmeister."

"Hockmeister is a grown man. He made a business decision and it turned out bad for him."

"He did, Mr. Orosco, but you don't seem to be giving him any credit for keeping his mouth shut. His family is suffering because of it."

Orosco's eyes suddenly flared with anger. He quickly took a step towards Jack and stabbed a finger into his chest. His voice was venomous. "Let me tell you something, Mister. Any man who puts the law onto me will regret it. People's houses have been known to burn down, sometimes with them inside it. Do you understand me?"

Jack could not hide his fear. His words were just short of quivering. "I do, Mr. Orosco. I understand completely."

"Good. I'll expect to see you in the morning with your friend."

Jack nodded. "I'll be here."

A disingenuous smile came over Orosco's face as he extended his hand. "Fine, no hard feelings."

Jack managed a weak grin, lest he not complete the charade, and shook Orosco's hand. "No, I'm good with $50 and gas."

It was clear to Phil and Siegler and no doubt Orosco that Jack wasn't good with things. It was a fact that like a wound unattended it would get worse, possibly turn gangrenous and have to be amputated.

For a time Jack drove the truck and neither of them spoke. They had been treated unfairly, as less than men even. From Phil's perspective, Jack had certainly gotten the worst of it. Things just hadn't gone as he'd thought they would. They were near the top of the dug-way road when he put it out there. "I didn't expect Orosco to be the way he is."

Jack allowed the truck to crest the hill and start across the mesa before looking at Phil. "I lied to you about Orosco giving me a beef. He took it out of my wages."

"Why did you lie about that?"

"I didn't think you'd sign on with Orosco if you knew how he really is and I didn't know what else ta do for ya." Jack paused and purposely looked straight ahead, down the road, and then he went on. "Hell, maybe I was just tryin' ta make him out to be a decent guy so you wouldn't think poorly of me for associatin' with someone like that."

Phil sighed. "We're in the same boat, Jack. I don't see where either one of us can look down his nose at the other one."

"Well, just so ya know, I aim ta quit Orosco just as soon as I can but this damned hail storm hasn't helped things."

Phil nodded as he dug in his shirt pocket for his cigarettes. "I'm of the same thought but for now I reckon we don't have much choice but to cozy up to 'im."

"I'll tell ya though, if after all this business is done with and I ever catch Orosco off his place, I aim ta give him a thrashin' he'll never forget."

Phil grinned and shook a Lucky part way out of the pack. "Ya smokin'?"

CHAPTER NINE

For Ranger, sleep had come easy. Phil, on the other hand, had tortured dreams driving the road to Miles City and back over and over. He encountered untold numbers of bad men with guns who had shot at him and Revenuers that chased him down and threw him in jail. And to top it off, Orosco shorted him on his gas money. All of these events came to a head in the retreating darkness of dawn. They left him exhausted and on edge. Three cups of black coffee did little to improve things. On the way to Jack's place his fatigue, at times, overwhelmed his consciousness causing him to be temporarily confused as to where he was and what he was doing. But then his mind would clear bringing him back to reality, which wasn't good either as there was Martha pleading with him to stay in Lincoln. He sighed. *I shudda listened to her.*

Phil stopped his truck next to Jack's and got out. "C'mon Ranger dog." They'd taken only a few steps towards the house when Jack came out with a cup of coffee. He appeared rested. "Mornin, you look like you could use one ah Ruth Ann's scones with some butter and honey."

"Don't ya figure we oughta git on down the road?"

"The hell with 'em. Man's gotta eat."

Considering the way things had gone yesterday, Phil was a little surprised at Jack's defiant attitude. He came back. "Well that sounds real fine as the pickin's at my place this mornin' was kinda lean except the Ranger dog here ate purty good. But if it's all the same to ya, I'll just eat mine on the way."

Jack hesitated for a moment as if he was assessing Phil's response. "Alright, I'll be right back."

The mood seemed quiet and somber to Phil, perhaps reflecting the fact that Jack had a new run. Ruth Ann was the first to come out. She was dressed in a blue gingham skirt and rust colored blouse that was gathered smartly around her waist. She had two scones wrapped in a towel and a cup of coffee. She handed them to Phil. "Good morning, Mr. Caldwell. Are you sure I can't fix you some eggs to go with these?"

"Oh, no thank you, Ma'am. The scones will be plenty. I'm much obliged." He paused. "Did Jack mention that I'd like ta leave Ranger here today?"

"He did. We'll be glad to have him."

"Thank you, Ma' am." Phil knelt down next to Ranger and tusseled his ears. "Your gonna stay here today and play with Heckles. So you mind yer manners, ok?"

Jack suddenly reappeared from the house. As he approached Ruth Ann, Phil could see that tears had formed in her eyes. He turned to give them their time and began walking towards his truck. He was envious of Jack and the family he had. His mind was already heavy with sadness and anger over all that had happened to him in recent days and now this morning fear had shoved them to the side, until just now. As if he expected mercy, he said to himself, *Lord, my plate is full.* And then Jack shouted, "Well, I guess we better be off."

His tone struck Phil as being almost gleeful. *Maybe that's what having a woman can do for you.*

It was 7:55 when they arrived at Orosco's barn. Siegler was waiting out front. He looked at Jack and shouted, "Schneider, back your truck in. We'll load you first." And then he positioned himself to guide Jack into the barn.

Phil parked his truck and got out. Siegler glanced his way but feigned a preoccupation with loading Jack's truck and said nothing. Phil kept his eyes on Siegler long enough for him to acknowledge him in some way but he did not. Phil sighed. *Well, it ain't like I came here to socialize.*

The bed of Jack's truck was made of a sheet of tin a quarter inch thick. It was bolted to strap iron ribs that ran the length of the six foot long space. The entire bed was bordered by wooden sideboards three feet tall, which allowed for the hauling of sacks of grain or bales of hay or as was the case today, sacks of coal. But first, the important cargo was loaded.

Jack handed Phil a wrench. "There's six bolts that hold this tin down. We need ta take 'em out and slide the bed back to where we can get to the tank underneath."

Phil took the wrench. "I was wonderin' how you was gonna hide this stuff."

Within minutes, they had exposed the 50 gallon tank. It was long and rectangular so as to fit in between two of the ribs but shallow enough so that it would not be visible to a casual inspection. A valve that accepted a rubber hose had been installed on the underside of the tank. Quart jars, gallon jugs, kegs or whatever container the customer wanted could be filled from it. The total weight of the tank when filled was a little over 400 pounds, not enough to cause much sag in the tires if a load of moonshine were to be hauled without some other diversionary cargo like coal, but Orosco never allowed that to happen.

Siegler stepped out of the tack room holding the end of a hose. "Are you two ready?"

"Whenever you are," said Jack.

Siegler handed the end of the hose to Phil and went back into the tack room.

Jack nodded towards the tank. "Take the cap off and stick the hose in it."

Phil climbed onto the bed of the truck, balancing on the exposed ribs and inserted the hose in the tank. "Ok, let 'er come."

Jack stepped into the tack room and shouted. "Alright Siegler, turn it on."

The outlet from the storage tank in the loft was about 15 feet higher than the tank in the bed of Jack's truck, as a consequence, the moonshine flowed freely out of the 5/8 inch hose. Still, it would take some time to gravity feed 50 gallons, a fact that lulled Phil, as the tank watcher, into a sort of complacency about the process. Jack on the other hand had no excuse. He and Phil had been talking quietly when all of a sudden Phil noticed the moonshine was about a half inch below the opening. "Better shut 'er off, Jack."

"Hey Siegler, shut it off."

"Alright"

But to Phil's horror, the moonshine began to overflow the tank. "Oh shit, it's still coming. Didn't he hear you?"

"Quick, pull the hose out. Put yer thumb over the end of it."

Phil leaned towards the hose so as to grab it near the end. In his haste he fell through the naked metal ribbing smacking his face. "Sonovabitch."

"Git it, Phil"

"What the hell do ya think I'm doin'?"

Seconds metered by the inevitable wrath of Siegler ticked by before Phil, with a trickle of blood on his cheek, finally pulled himself up and got to the hose. But the damage had been done. Close to a gallon of moonshine had overflowed the tank onto the barn floor. Phil could hear Siegler climbing down the tack room wall. He looked at Jack with fear in his eyes.

"I'll deal with Siegler," said Jack.

"Alright, start dealin'."

Jack and Phil looked over their shoulders to see Siegler standing in the open doorway of the tack room. He appeared angry as he stepped over to the bed of the truck. It took only an instant for him to deduce what had happened because this wasn't the first time that someone hadn't accounted for the residual liquid in the hose to flow out after it's shut off. Nonetheless, he scoffed. "You two shitbirds can't even be trusted to fill the tank and here we are sending you off to deliver it." He shook his head while looking at Phil. "I figure you ran about $20 worth ah shine onto the dirt. That's gonna come outta your pay."

"It ain't his fault," said Jack. "I shudda warned him. I just forgot. You can take it outta my pay"

"That's mighty noble of you," said Siegler sarcastically, "but the cost of that shine is coming out of your friend's wages."

Phil jumped into the fray. "It's alright, Jack. I shudda been keepin' ah better eye on things."

Siegler looked at Phil, a little surprised and then turned to Jack. "See, he knows he's wrong." He then deliberately paused while looking Jack hard in the face as if to dare him to continue the argument. Jack pulled in his anger and went quiet. Siegler smirked. "Alright, you two get the bed put back on this truck and load it and the other truck with coal. Put 15 sacks on each truck." Siegler came back to Phil. "I'll tell you this cuz Schneider here seems to have forgotten how things work." He pointed toward the stalls at the front of the barn. "Each one of those sacks of coal has a gallon jug in it. So, unless you wanna buy some more shine you and your friend will handle those sacks real careful like."

Phil didn't appreciate being talked down to. It was an effort for him to control his anger, nonetheless he came back respectful of where he was and the fact he needed money. "Alright, I believe we can do that."

Siegler laughed as he walked away. "I guess we'll see."

Phil looked hatefully at Siegler's back. When he was certain that Siegler had started up the wall to the loft, he whispered, "What an asshole."

Jack grinned but then in the next instant he became serious. "It's who he is. We just need ta git the coal loaded and leave."

It took slightly less than a half hour to do as Siegler had asked. The trucks were parked in front of the barn, loaded and ready to go. Phil and Jack were standing next to them looking towards Orosco's house as if they were waiting for water to come to a boil. Phil had lit a Lucky Strike. He was conscious of the impression it might give Siegler but the need to take the edge off of how things had gone thus far trumped that concern. He took a drag of his cigarette and blew the smoke down and to the side. "So what happens now?"

"Wait. He knows we're here."

"Why don't we just go up there and ask him?"

"I've been doing this almost a year and I've never been in that house."

Phil nodded. "Oh." Across the yard, perched high up in a pine tree, a Stellar's jay began to screech. "Orosco got a wife and kids?"

Jack glanced around to see if Siegler or anyone else might be within earshot. Seeing no one, he came back. "Yeah, he's got a wife and two kids. She's here. I see her putterin' ever once in a while in them flowers she's got planted around the house. But the kids, I guess they went off to school and just never come back. One ah the cowpuncher hands told me he's seen 'em at Christmas but no other times and he's spent a good part of his life here."

"I ain't never had kids but I suspect that wouldn't sit too well."

"I guess it was just too much solitude for 'em."

Phil took another drag of his cigarette. "Maybe they couldn't stomach their pa."

All of a sudden, Jack's eyes widened and reached out to the house. "Here he comes. I'd put that smoke out if I was you."

Phil frowned and shook his head before tossing the cigarette down and grinding it into the ground with the toe of his boot. As Orosco got closer he tried to gauge his temperament. There were no beginnings of a smile as a prelude to saying *good morning* but rather his outward demeanor suggested he was already angry about something. When he was within loud conversation distance, Jack called out. "Mornin' Mr. Orosco."

It was like Orosco hadn't heard Jack. He just kept coming while probing his shirt pocket for a piece of paper. When he was directly in front of Jack, he stopped and held the paper out.

"Here's a list of where you'll deliver to in Bismarck. These are new customers. I think the Feds somehow got onto where Hockmeister was making his stops so we ain't goin' to those places anymore. They pinched him at a place called the Red Rooster Supper Club so stay clear of it."

The angst that had begun brewing within Jack ever since he learned he was to replace Hockmeister suddenly boiled over like an unattended kettle of mash. He sighed real deep and then came back. "Mr. Orosco, this whole deal in Bismarck sounds to me like it could be another General Custer debacle. You know the damned Feds are just waitin' on us to come back."

Anger impulsively flared in Orosco's eyes before he could catch himself, but then seeing how Jack was and knowing that he had no one else to go in his place, he reined it in. "You'll be alright. Your load is well disguised."

"That won't matter if the Feds are watchin' these places. I don't feel good about this."

"So you're just gonna leave me high and dry? I was countin' on you."

"Well, I –"

"I'll tell ya what. I'll give you $20 for a room and meals. Anything left over is yours."

It wasn't like Jack hadn't thought of it before but it was now a reality that he could make some serious money if he were to sleep in the truck and go easy on the food. However, it suddenly occurred to him that maybe he had some leverage over this man who had been dictating to him how things would be for the past year. He was emboldened. "Mr. Orosco, we spilled ah little shine this morning. Siegler wants Phil to pay $20 for it. If you'd be willin' ta write that off and still allow me $20 for ah room and meals, I'll make the trip to Bismarck."

A subdued anger rose up in Orosco's face. He laughed briefly in a derisive, hateful way while staring at Jack. He then glanced at Phil and snorted as if to imply he was incompetent. "Alright Schneider, you've got the better of me today. Now be on your way"

Jack thought to thank Orosco but he did not. Instead he turned to Phil. "I'll see you in a coupla days."

Phil was preoccupied with what Jack had just done for him. "Thanks Jack. I appreciate it." From the corner of his eye he could see Orosco bristle. He went on. "Keep ah sharp watch for the Feds."

Jack smiled weakly, kind of like he was still doomed to ride with Custer. "I aim to." And then he started for his truck.

"Mr. Caldwell, you're burnin' daylight."

Phil turned quickly toward Orosco.

"Your job is simple. Just deliver the bags of coal to the Yellowstone Mercantile in Miles City. Ask for Mr. Orwell, he's the proprietor."

"That's it. I don't collect any money for the shine."

"That's not your concern."

"Ok." Phil paused as if he had something else to say.

"I'll mail you your money once I know you've made the delivery. Might be a week."

Phil looked doubtful, if not annoyed. He just wasn't comfortable with Orosco and definitely not Siegler. Once he was away from here, he wondered if he would ever come back. He knew as sure as he was standing there now that he wanted to cut his ties with this man, but if he was to ever find out about Martha he would have to return and that meant risking his freedom and his truck for fifty dollars.

Orosco smirked indignantly. "Do you not trust me?"

"I do. I guess I was just wanting to be clear on how things worked."

"Well, now you know. Did Mr. Siegler give you a key to the gate?"

"Yes sir."

"Well then, there's nothing to keep you here."

Phil stood still, the indecision in his mind not allowing him to move.

"Alright Mr. Caldwell, what the hell is troubling you?"

Phil looked at Orosco. What little patience he might have had this morning had been exhausted by Jack's negotiations. He wasn't used to not having things his way. Phil knew it wasn't a good time but he reckoned, *why would a man want to go into a den full of rattlesnakes more than once.* His heart suddenly began to pound as he blindsided Orosco with it. "A man abducted my wife a short time back. I believe he came through your land. Would you have any knowledge of who he might be?"

Orosco was clearly taken by surprise. He hesitated long enough to ready himself so as to sound convincing. "I have no idea what in the hell you are talking about."

In his impulsive naiveté, Phil had not prepared a challenge to Orosco's denial. It was like he'd thrown a weak left jab and Orosco had countered it with a right cross that stunned him. He was not certain what Orosco might be capable of if threatened, especially here behind locked gates on his own land. He came back, leaving Orosco an out. "Is there any way across your place that a man could travel and you might not see him?"

"Not by automobile, there's not. Hell, even a man on foot I doubt wouldn't get by my hands. They're always out checking on the cattle and fences and water and such."

Phil hoped that his eyes hadn't given him away and that his mind had locked the door on his thoughts. *The sonovabitch is lyin' as sure as the sun comes up in the east.* He came back, thinking maybe he could at least cause Orosco to worry or if he was lucky, suddenly remember something.

"Well, the Sheriff is lookin' into it. Maybe he'll come up with something."

Orosco laughed. "Hell, Wylie Hargis is lucky to find his way home."

Phil nodded. He'd been stupid to think Orosco would ever be forthright with him, not even if he called him a liar. He came back as if he'd lost interest in their conversation. "I reckon I better be on my way."

"Yes, you should. Just so you know, if this trip is satisfactory and I desire for you to make another, I'll let you know that when I send your money."

"Alright, I'll wait ta hear from ya."

The road to Miles City actually required Phil to backtrack through Orosco's property and down the wooded coulee to the main road into town. From Baker it would be about a three hour drive to Miles City, but before he could start on this leg of his trip he needed gas. He was parked in front of the Baker Mercantile pumping his fuel when he heard a car pull up behind him. At first, he paid no attention to it. He was focused on cranking the handle to pump his gas and watching the gallon meter click away and doing the math of how much he would owe at 22 cents a gallon.

"Mornin' Mr. Caldwell."

Phil turned around with a start. Right away his eyes locked onto the gold star on the door of the big black car, but only for a second, as standing there next to it was Wiley Hargis. Even though he'd already checked them, paranoia caused him to glance over at the sacks of coal. They were all intact. He continued cranking the gas pump but made eye contact with Wiley. "Mornin' Sheriff."

Wiley came closer, his eyes fixed on Phil's load of coal. "Takin' up ah new line ah work are ya?"

Right away Phil thought back to him and the Sheriff's conversation about the choices people might make following the big hail storm. His heart began to throb as his eyes came back to the sacks of coal. *Ain't no way he could know and he ain't got the right tu open them bags,* he said to himself. And then, as he looked at the Sheriff, another one of Miss Maricelli's platitudes popped into his mind, *one lie begets another.* He came back with part of the truth, "Yes sir, I am. I'm haulin' some coal over to Miles City for Mr. Orosco. He's got ah little coal diggin' operation on his place."

"Makin' it worth your while is he?"

And just like that, Phil felt the jaws of the Sheriff's trap snap shut. There'd be no escape from it unless he came up with a plausible answer and $50 and gas wasn't it nor was, *it's none ah yer business* as these answers might arouse the Sheriff's suspicion enough to want to open the sacks. He was still doing the math when the Sheriff grinned and came again. "Mr. Orosco musta found his self ah fool over there in Miles City to sell his coal to."

At this point, Phil knew he had no option but to play stupid. "How's that?"

"Last I heard, coal was goin' for a nickel ah pound. It don't seem ta me like this little jag you got here would be profitable to haul all the way to Miles City."

And so Phil told his first lie, hoping that a second wouldn't be necessary. "I guess Mr. Orosco made this deal before the price of coal went down. I can assure you though, I ain't gittin' rich on this and I most likely won't be subjectin' my truck to the wear and tear of a second trip."

The Sheriff rested his forearms on the side of Phil's truck bed for a moment before reaching over and feeling one of the sacks.

Phil's heart nearly exploded as he struggled to keep his voice steady. "No sir, ah second trip just wouldn't be worth it."

The Sheriff nodded and stepped back from the truck. "I would say that's probably a real wise choice." He then looked Phil straight in the eye and grinned. "Have a nice trip."

There was no doubt in Phil's mind that Wiley Hargis knew what was in the sacks, yet here he was walking away and into the Mercantile to get a sarsaparilla.

CHAPTER TEN

The trip to Miles City did not measure up to Phil's worst fears, for other than Wiley Hargis he did not encountered a single lawman. Nonetheless, he wasn't going to allow himself to become cocky and think that he had gotten away with anything. The look on Wiley's face as he felt of the coal sack that day in front of the Mercantile had become permanently fixed in Phil's mind. *I'd be ah damned fool ta try an' sneak another load ah coal over there.* And so it was he'd reconciled himself to waiting till his money arrived and then, unless he was overcome by stupidity, he was just going to mail Orosco's gate key back to him.

It was close to noon on the third day after he'd returned. The sun was unmercifully hot which made it all the more peculiar that someone would be walking up the road to his place, unless their reason for doing so was pretty important. Phil raised both hands palms down as an extension to the brim of his hat so as to be able to see better. Way out there, the heat was such it distorted things. It made them appear to be quivering like the incessant waves of a flag blowing in the wind. However, after a short while he recognized the cream colored straw hat, red cotton shirt and bib overalls as belonging to Orville Schneider. He instantly whispered. "Ah shit." And although Orville was walking briskly, it took him another couple of minutes before he was close enough to shout out. "They got Pa in jail."

Phil could see the rivulets of sweat running down the reddened face of the boy. Orville, still walking and breathing heavily, came again. "The Sheriff brought word to us this morning. Ma is beside herself."

Phil grimaced and sighed. "C'mon outta the sun, I've got some cool water."

Orville followed Phil and Ranger inside Phil's little shanty. A two gallon sized metal bucket full of water sat on the counter to the left of the door. Phil nodded towards the bucket. "Help yerself to ah drink."

Orville quickly took up the tin ladle that was resting beside the bucket and scooped up some water. He began to drink in a noisy, breathy kind of way, like he was desperate for the water. His hunger for it was such that not all of it made it into his mouth. After his third ladle full there were moist trails running from the corners of his mouth down to his jawbones, but his thirst appeared satisfied. He set the ladle on the plank counter and turned to Phil who had taken a seat at the table. He began again, kind of where he'd left off outside. "The Sheriff says Pa likely won't git out of jail for six months."

"Six months." And then Phil reined in his shock so as to not make the boy's fear worse and nodded towards the empty chair across from him. "Sit yerself down."

Orville pulled the chair out from the table allowing it to make a prolonged scraping noise on the wooden floor. As he sat down he went on. "They took Pa's truck too. The Sheriff says if we want it back we'll have to buy it at an auction. Ma started cryin' when she heard that."

Phil's mind flashed back to the day in front of Orosco's barn when Jack had voiced his concern that going to Bismarck now would be akin to riding with Custer. He sighed as he knew what the probable expectation of him would now be. *Dammit, Jack knew things were likely to go bad and he went right on ahead and did it. It's his own fault.* And then in the next instant his conscience reminded him of all that Jack had done for him and that he had concluded Wiley Hargis was smarter than folks gave him credit for and that he was lucky to not be sitting in the Fallon County jail. His shame was quick and caused him to come back. "Is yer Ma needin' help? Is that why you walked all the way out here?"

Orville nodded. "She's hopin' you'll take her to see Mr. Orosco."

"I don't mean to dash yer Ma's hopes but I don't think he will help."

"She knows how he is but she says nobody is that heartless."

Phil scoffed. "I don't know about that, Orville."

Orville sighed as if he agreed. "It's what Ma wants."

"When does she want to go there?"

"Now, I reckon. She's got herself pretty worked up."

"What about you? How's all this sittin' with you?"

"Pa says cryin' won't fix anything, but I still feel like it."

Phil thought of his time in the well. He'd cried hard and nobody came to help him, at least not right then, except Ranger. But, for a little while, it had drained off some of his fear. He looked at Orville as if there was some room for doubt in what his Pa had told him. "Maybe you should save yer cryin' for a private time. Be easier on yer Ma that way."

Orville looked at Phil still uncertain as to what to do with the advice he'd just been given. "What should I tell Ma? Will you take her to Mr. Orosco's?"

It was about a ten minute ride to the Schneider house. Based on Ruth Ann's appearance when Phil and Orville arrived, it had been a foregone conclusion with her that she and Phil would continue on to Orosco's. She was wearing a blue and yellow paisley dress that was gathered with a black belt at her waist and a white straw hat with a burgundy ribbon around the base of its crown. It was the best she had to wear. Her lips were painted a bright red as was the style with some city girls. It was a stretch, at least to Phil it was, to say she was beautiful but she was comely and would turn most men's heads made up as she was. Pete Orosco, however, was not like most men.

Phil could not bring himself to talk common sense or logic to Ruth Ann. It would have been akin to locking her in a dark box with nothing but her sorrow and not allowing the lid to be cracked even the slightest bit. He couldn't do that to her but suspected Pete Orosco could.

"Now Orville, you watch out for your sister and don't either one of you leave the place. We'll be home by supper time." And then Ruth Ann turned to Phil for confirmation. "We will won't we, Mr. Caldwell?"

"I suspect we will."

Ruth Ann took a step towards her kids with the intention of giving them a hug, but stopped suddenly when she felt tears coming on her. She did an about face that seemed odd to the others there but yet it needed no explanation. "Shall we go, Mr. Caldwell?"

Phil nodded and opened the door of his truck for her. Ruth Ann climbed in and sat down being careful to pull all of her long dress in before Phil shut the door. She called out, as if her kids were mischievous, which they weren't, "You two behave yourselves while I'm gone." Phil fired up his truck and then amidst the noise of the engine and Ranger and

Heckles barking, Ruth Ann said what she'd wanted to say all along. "I love the both of you."

And then they were off, back to the main road where Phil turned north towards the wooded coulee two-track and Orosco's. For a mile or so Ruth Ann was profuse in her appreciation of what Phil was doing for her and in similar fashion he reminded her of all that she and Jack had done for him and how it was the least he could do until, finally, a silence started to descend over them. Ruth Ann, however, was resistant to it.

"These are certainly hard times, Mr. Caldwell. Don't you think?"

"Yes Ma'am, they are."

"First your Martha is taken away and now my Jack."

Phil dared not look at Ruth Ann, as a spark of incredulous anger had suddenly come into his eyes. "But you can take some comfort in knowing where Jack is at and that he will be coming home to you. The same can't be said for Martha as she is most likely dead."

If she recognized her faux pas as such, Ruth Ann did not take ownership of it. She went on. "The Sheriff hasn't learned anything knew?"

"Not to my knowledge he hasn't."

And then Ruth Ann got to the crux of what was really on her mind. "Jack tells me my suspicions are just the makings of women's gossip but I think not."

"What are you talking about?"

"Edith Walters, she's behaved oddly about this whole affair with Martha."

"How's that?"

"Everybody that I've talked to about this is truly shocked by it. My sense of Edith is she's pretending."

"Pretending?"

"Yes, like she was expecting this to happen."

Phil sighed and shook his head. "I don't know why that would be, but I do know the woman is not being truthful about who she saw go by her place."

"It's all very peculiar. As close as she was to Martha I just thought she would be more concerned."

"She was close to Martha?"

"Yes, at our book club meetings the two of them appeared to share a confidence that the rest of us were not privy to."

Phil frowned in a quizzical sort of way. "I don't recall Martha ever talking about Edith like she was a real friend, but I suppose she might talk to someone about how it was between us."

The last of Phil's words struck a chord with Ruth Ann causing her to ease up in the direction she was going. "Well maybe Jack's right and it's just my imagination at work."

Phil sighed. "I don't know. I just don't know what to make of it."

They drove on up the wooded coulee, across the broad grassy mesa and were part way down the dug-way road when Phil looked over at Ruth Ann so as to make eye contact. "Orosco's likely not going to be pleased we're here so it's probably best if I do the talking to start with."

The brashness that had been so abundant in Ruth Ann when they'd first started out had seemingly drained away like the sands of an hour glass. She now appeared fearful and nervous. "That's probably best, Mr. Caldwell, but he's just got to help us. I have nowhere else to turn to."

Phil made no response. He'd warned her of what to expect and there was no sugar coating that now.

Orosco and Siegler had watched them come down the hill. They were waiting in front of the barn. It was clear to Phil that Orosco sensed trouble because of Ruth Ann being there and had already taken on an angry look. The noise of the truck's engine had not quite died away when Orosco shouted over it. "Mr. Caldwell, did you not understand my instructions? I told you that I would mail you your money. Unnecessary trips out here will only draw attention to our business arrangement and that, if detected by the wrong people, will end it for the both of us. I was hoping that you were smarter than that."

Phil wanted to fire back at Orosco but knew better. "I'm sorry Sir but I've come on another matter."

"He's here because of me, I'm Jack Schneider's wife." said Ruth Ann in a timid voice.

Orosco's eyes appeared to glisten in a mean way as if he relished the power he held over Phil and Ruth Ann. His tone was sarcastic. "So why have you come here?"

"Don't you know? Jack's in jail."

"Yes, and I've lost an entire load of moonshine."

"You can always make more."

"And Jack can just do the time. I doubt that it will be too long."

"Six months and they took our truck and they fined him $250. Losing our truck and Jack being in jail and not able to work is bad enough, but there's just no way we can come up with $250."

"Well, I made it clear to Jack how things would be if he were ever to get caught and he signed on anyway. So, I feel no obligation to go back now and change that."

Ruth Ann's look became hateful. "The Sheriff has told me if Jack were to tell them who he was hauling moonshine for that they would drop the fine and give us our truck back and maybe let him out of jail in a month. Let me tell you Mr. Orosco, as a mother with two kids to feed and a note at the bank coming due this fall that all sounds very tempting."

Orosco's face turned red with anger. He took a step towards Ruth Ann and then stared hard into her eyes. "Now you listen to me, you senseless bitch."

"Watch yer mouth."

Instantly, Orosco turned his wrath on Phil. "You fool, have you forgotten where you're at? I could bury both of you out here and nobody would ever know."

Phil's anger at that very moment was greater than his fear of Orosco. Still, he had an awareness about him that those scales could tip the other way at any time, it caused him to go on quickly before they did. "Mr. Orosco, I think it is you who is the fool. You can't treat people this way and expect others to step up for more of the same. It'll be the end of yer moonshine business unless yer gonna drive the loads yerself and I don't see that happening as I don't think you've got the moxie for it."

Orosco glared at Phil as if he was just so much nothingness unworthy of his attention. "No Caldwell, when this is all over I'll have what I do now and you will have nothing because your kind has never had anything in life and never will. So, take your friend here and get the hell off of my land and I promise you, if you ever attempt to play this blackmail chip again it will be the end for the both of you."

Phil had not expected Orosco to respond as he had. His words were prophetic; perhaps too close to the reason Phil had come to this land in the first place. They gutted his anger. He came back, almost respectful. "I've got money comin'."

Orosco grinned in a smug way. He said, nodding towards Ruth Ann, "You come here with this hussie makin' threats and now you want your money." He paused looking straight at Ruth Ann but she held her tongue. After a moment, he went on looking almost disappointed that she'd not taken the bait. "I'm of a mind to just send your ass ah packin'."

"I suppose you could but that wouldn't be right."

Orosco paused as if his conscience was talking to him. Finally, he shook his head and sighed before reaching for his wallet. He took out some bills and handed them to Phil saying nothing as he did.

"There's only $32 here."

"That's right. $30 wages less $20 for the shine you spilled and $2 for gas."

"That's not what we agreed to."

"The product your friend lost in Bismarck cost me about $1,300. I gotta make that up somewhere."

Phil scoffed. "So ya aim to start by gouging me for twenty dollars."

"I'm done with you. Now get off my land. And you can leave my key under a rock by the gate post on your way out. You won't have need for it anymore."

For a few seconds Phil stood where he was frantically searching his mind for some bit of leverage that he could apply on behalf of Ruth Ann, but there was none. Nor was there anything that he could say in personal retaliation to a man whose moral compass was so flawed. The trip, to use Jack's analogy, had been a ride with Custer.

CHAPTER ELEVEN

Phil did not stay for supper. He needed to be away from all that had happened, if that was possible. The return trip had been somber, almost taking on the feel that they'd just attended a funeral. To her credit, Ruth Ann held back her tears until they were well south of Orosco's house and then she began to sob, mostly quiet and to herself but, at times, it became loud as if that would take away her sadness. They had talked little, as other than money there was no good fix to their situation.

It was half past seven. Phil had not been home long. He'd just fed Ranger his usual dog chow and was sitting on an old wooden chair in front of his shanty smoking a cigarette. He was resting his elbows on his knees, alternately looking down at the ants near his boots trying to make sense of their coming and going and then up and out to the east towards the main road and all of the choppy hills and coulees between them. It was soothing to watch the shadows begin to take hold of the land and to listen as Ranger munched his way through his food. He was hungry himself but he just couldn't bring himself to build a fire in the stove and cook. After all that had happened that day, just doing nothing and soaking up the silence felt good. But then off in the distance he could hear a car coming. He looked up from the ants and immediately recognized it as belonging to Miss Maricelli. Lately, it had come to him, mostly in the night when his loneliness was at its worst, that if Martha never came back he would court Miss Maricelli. But then the naysayer that never left his mind cast shame on him. *Martha ain't even cold in the ground and here you are lookin' ta put ah new heifer in yer pen.* And then the naysayer laughed at him in a cruel, mocking sort of way before going on. *Besides, what can you offer a woman like that, yer a failure.*

Ranger cast a wary eye toward the approaching car but continued to eat. As it worked out, he finished his supper just as the car came to a stop in front of him and Phil. He ran to greet Miss Maricelli, barking as he went. "Oh, hi to you too, Ranger."

Phil stood up. "Evenin' Ma'am."

"Good evening, Mr. Caldwell. I thought you might like a rhubarb pie. Do you care for it? A lot of people don't but it grows in abundance up at my spring."

Phil lied. "It's one of my favorites."

Catarina was dressed in loose fitting brown cotton pants, cowboy boots and a long sleeved burnt orange shirt with the sleeves rolled up to the elbows. She held the pie out to Phil. "You'll have to excuse my appearance. I've been working in my garden today."

Phil's thoughts at that moment were floating close to the surface and they escaped him. "You always look real fine to me, Ma'am, regardless of yer attire."

Catarina blushed as did Phil causing their meeting to suddenly become awkward but deep down, not unwelcome. Phil took the pie and quickly looked away so as to avoid eye contact. He left his words hanging in the air. "Come inside, we'll cut a piece."

"Thank you, Mr. Caldwell that would be a fine way to conclude the day."

Phil went through the open door followed by Catarina and Ranger. He set the pie on the counter and then quickly moved to the table and pulled a chair out for her. "I can make us a cup a coffee ta go with the pie if ya like?"

Catarina glanced at the stove. It was quiet and appeared cold. "I believe a glass of water would do for me if that's ok."

Phil thought to be overly hospitable and offer up the coffee again but it was already warm in the shanty. He felt some guilt but nonetheless, he came back, "Alright, water it'll be." He took two glasses from the shelf above the water bucket and then using the same ladle that earlier Orville had drunk from, which now seemed so long ago, he scooped up their drinks. He could feel Catarina watching him as he set the glasses on the table. It was not outright staring but rather it was indirect and subtle. He returned to the counter and began cutting the pie. "How big a piece do ya want?"

"Oh, not too big."

Phil's mind instantly went to those times when he'd dished up something for Martha after she had given him similar directions that were imprecise. Unlike now, he'd come back with, *well what's not too big?* But things were different now so he cut a piece a little smaller than his. He set the plates of pie with forks on the table and then sat down.

"Bon appetit, Mr. Caldwell."

Phil had heard that expression before but wasn't quite sure what it meant. He came back. "Sure looks good."

"I hope so."

They began to eat with Phil straight away confirming how good the pie was and Catarina thanking him for the compliment and him thanking her for bringing the pie until suddenly they had exhausted the social pleasantries that were germane to their being together and they were left with the white elephants that haunted the room. Catarina went first, she was blunt. "So will you be able to hang on for another year?"

"I don't know how. The hail, the damned hail wiped me out."

"Me too."

"But you have your teacher's salary."

Catarina smiled derisively. "Not if the people who have kids move away. There'll be no need for a school."

"Do you think that will happen?"

"It could. I've already heard of a couple of families who are giving up and leaving."

"I'm sorry to hear that. What will you do?"

"I don't know. I don't want to give up but if there's no school I don't know how I can make it here. And you, will you go back to Lincoln?"

"No, there would be too many memories there. And besides, I don't want to leave here until all of this business with Martha is resolved."

"Is there anything new in that regard?"

Phil shook his head. "No, but I am convinced that Edith Walters knows more about this whole affair than she is letting on."

Catarina did not question Phil's assertion. "She does seem uncomfortable when the subject of Martha's disappearance comes up."

"Ruth Ann tells me kind of the same thing."

"It may be that it is hurtful to her. She and Martha were close."

Phil sighed. "Maybe so, but it seems more than that."

And then an awkward silence fell over the room punctuated only by the ticking of the alarm clock near the bed. "I suppose I should go. The neighbors see my car over here this late and they'll no doubt conjure up a scandal to ward off the boredom of their lives."

Catarina was suddenly on her feet and had taken a step towards the door before Phil could stand. "Thanks again for the pie. It was real tasty."

She did not look back but said over her shoulder, "You're most welcome."

Phil followed her outside. "Maybe we can talk again. I've got some thoughts on our financial problems."

Catarina stopped and turned. "Why didn't you bring them up tonight?"

Phil appeared to be mute, finally he said, "It's a topic that needs more thinkin' on my part."

Catarina made a face as if she was slightly annoyed at being teased. "Well, if you ever get that done, I guess you know the way to my place."

Phil smiled weakly. "I expect ta git it sorted out soon. Time isn't on my side."

Catarina started again for her car. "Nor mine, Mr. Caldwell. Have a good night."

He waved as her car rolled by and then he stood and watched as she got farther and farther away until finally her headlights disappeared behind the ridge that separated them. Phil sighed. He hated the night as sleep did not come easy anymore. "C'mon, Ranger dog." And in the darkness they resumed their places in front of the shanty.

CHAPTER TWELVE

There were meadow larks singing, several of them, from the sagebrush skeletons that surrounded his decimated grain field. He'd wrestled with the proposition throughout the night and now here he was at dawn walking the land that had cost him his wife. It and the powers that ruled it had not been kind or maybe even fair to him. He was uncertain if it was worth any more of his life. At first he thought he would just go it alone, but there was nothing covert about his place. It just seemed too naked for that kind of thing. Jack's place had come to mind but he was already in jail and under suspicion. And then he came to where he knew all along he had wanted to go, but to ask someone to purposely skew their moral compass in such a way could be taken as an insult. There could be a heavy price to pay. Nonetheless, he'd committed to think it out and then come see her.

He figured nine o'clock would be a respectable hour so until then he drank coffee and even had a couple of plate size sourdough hotcakes with some of her chokecherry preserves and butter on them. At last it was time. In the powdery dirt he could see her tracks from the night before. They were sharp and well defined, like it was their purpose to keep him from straying. He followed them to just short of where she had parked next to her little shack.

"Good morning."

Phil looked over to his left. Catarina was just coming out of the chicken coop with a small wicker basket full of eggs. He hollered back, "Mornin' Ma'am," and then slid out of his truck followed by Ranger and began walking towards her.

They approached one another until they were close enough that they could gage the tenor of what the other was thinking or going to say by the look in their eyes. Catarina stopped first. She smiled. "So, have you completed your financial pondering?"

"Well, I guess I have."

Catarina continued to smile. "You don't sound too certain of that."

"I thought I was until I got here."

"I'm sorry."

"Don't be. It's just me. I can never make up my mind for sure."

"Is that how you came to be a homesteader?"

A pulse of anger went through Phil as she had seen right away what some people never did. "I don't know. Were you sure this was what you wanted to do?"

"Yes, but I'm that way. When I decide to do something I don't second guess myself."

"Alright, this otta be purty cut an' dried for ya. Whaddaya think about goin' into the moonshine business with me?"

Mild shock was her first response but only for a moment and then Catarina began to laugh. "Why yes, Mr. Caldwell that sounds like a grand idea, a fine solution to our financial problems. I suspect that we could sell all that we make to Mr. Capone in Chicago." And then she began to laugh even harder until she saw that Phil was serious whereupon she suddenly stopped. "You really want to do this don't you?"

"I do. I've had a taste of this business already. It's not without risk-"

"I know. I read the paper. People are going to jail every week."

"It's because the money to be made is insanely good. Three or four trips and our money problems will be solved."

"Trips? To where?"

"I'm not certain. Maybe Miles City."

Catarina paused, her eyes now looking over Phil as if he were somebody she didn't know. "Why are you asking me to do this? Of all people why me? I know nothing about making moonshine whiskey or where to sell it."

During his thinking last night it had not seemed fair to ask this of her, but he could not let go of it as there was some logic to it. And there were other feelings too that he tried to pretend did not exist. Phil came back. "That's exactly why. Nobody will suspect you, the schoolmarm? Who would think such a thing?"

And then it suddenly came to her. It was as if someone had lit a match in a dark room. "You want to locate the still at my place, don't you? It's because you think the law will never come to my house."

Phil was embarrassed. She had called it as it was and there was no putting distance between that fact and his self. But truth be told, he was beginning to care for her as a friend and maybe more. She had been kind to him, bringing him food these past few weeks. He sighed. "I know it doesn't look good. I'd put the still at my place or Jack's but – well, Jack's already in jail and I've gotten crosswise with-"

"Jack Schneider is in jail? Oh, poor Ruth Ann and the kids. How did this happen?"

"He was delivering shine over in Bismarck. I don't know how the Feds got on to him but he's in the hoosgow over there for the next six months."

"And you've gotten crosswise with someone?"

"Yes, I'll tell you but you can never pass on to anyone who this person is or what he's doing."

"This kind of talk scares me. Maybe I shouldn't know who it is?"

"If we don't throw in together makin' shine there is no need for you to know. But if we do, you should know who my enemies are and I suppose the competition."

"This man makes moonshine?"

"He does and I aim to undercut his price."

"Sounds to me like you'll be inviting trouble. Why would you want to do that?"

"The man is a heartless scoundrel."

"Aren't you afraid of what might happen to you?"

"Yeah, it worries me some but it was *his* customer who was grousin' about the price. Said he might start buyin' from Canadian bootleggers. Said he could save himself three dollars a gallon. So either we sell it to him or the Canadians will. Either way, my old boss is out of luck."

Catarina sighed and looked to the south and the field that Phil had broken out and planted for her this past spring. The wheat had been hammered down by the hail and now it lay on the ground, brown and rotting. The practical side of her said she should steer clear of this radical idea and this man who was embracing it out of desperation and that she should go to Denver, live with her sister, and get a job teaching. But that option had been open to her when she had chosen to become a homesteader. She turned back to Phil and smiled. "So who is this man you're crosswise with?"

Phil's first thought was to ask her; *Are you sure you want to do this*? But it was plain there was no need. "His name is Pete Orosco. He owns the big place to the east of us."

"You worked for this man?"

"I did, just briefly. He's not a fair person."

Catarina laughed as if they were discussing a school prank. "I can't believe we're actually talking of doing something illegal."

Phil's expression was carved from stone. "We are and no one can know. The slightest indiscretion could land us in jail."

"It occurs to me that all of these people that have been caught probably started out just as we are and then over time there was some little mistake that caused them to be discovered."

Phil snorted as if to underscore what Catarina had said and nodded his head in an emphatic way. "They did and they got caught because they didn't know when to stop."

"And we do?"

"I just want to make enough so I can stay on for another year and help the Schneider's out some. When that time comes, I'm done."

Catarina studied Phil's face for a moment. She said in an earnest voice; "I have similar objectives, Mr. Caldwell, and I believe what you just said but greed lurks in the heart of every person, including us. We need to be ever mindful of that and not allow it to get the better of us."

Phil absorbed what she had said. "Down the line we need to remind one another of this talk."

Catarina nodded and began walking. "I've got coffee inside."

CHAPTER THIRTEEN

It had been two days since they'd drank coffee together. In that time, Phil had done more thinking, his homework so to speak. It had come to him that as bad as the big hail storm was, it had somehow missed the coulee to the west of Catarina's where the spring was located and in so doing it also granted a reprieve to this year's chokecherry crop. This was fortuitous as was the fact that her chickens had shown the good sense to abandon their fenced in run and ride out the storm within the confines of their coop. There had been a point in his thinking where he had considered Catarina the benefactor of divine intervention, being the schoolmarm and all, but after a time he dismissed this notion in favor of it was just luck of the draw. There were some chickens in the area that had been caught out in the open and beaten by the hail in an unmerciful manner until they were dead and good to no one except those people who discovered them in time to salvage their carcasses. But this misfortune had not befallen Catarina. She was grateful and Phil too as these chance events would accommodate their plans nicely.

It was true they were now on a first name basis and had agreed, or at least earlier that morning they had, to ride into town in Phil's truck as a way to save gas money. But now Baker was in sight and in a few minutes the schoolmarm and the most likely recently widowed neighbor of hers would be visible to all for their moral assessment. Catarina was first to address the paranoia that resided within the both of them. "I hope this is not a mistake."

"It makes sense, Catarina. Times are hard."

"You know how people are. They don't need much provocation to gossip and once it starts there is no stopping it."

Phil took his eyes from the road and looked purposely at her so as to be able to gage the effects of what he was about to say. "I have no doubt there will be folks who are going to speculate on where I park my boots at night." Catarina instantly blushed, but she did not look away. Phil continued. "I suspect those same people are going to pass judgement on me as some immoral scoundrel being seen with a single woman when the disposition of my own wife is not known for certain. I can't say that I don't care what people think about me or us, but today is just a consequence of the times we live in. Our reputations are just going to have to weather the storm. I'm sorry."

Catarina sighed, her facial muscles frowning slightly. The boldness with which she had entered their business arrangement two days ago had withered away under the scrutiny of prolonged thought. She came back. "I've got a reputation to maintain."

Phil brought the truck to a stop and looked at her. His voice was stern. "I can turn around 'fore any of the busybodies in town see us. I'll take ya home and we'll just scuttle this whole idea."

Catarina grimaced and shook her head. "I guess I'm just scared."

"Well, it's not like I ain't got my concerns too. But to be honest, I worry less about my reputation than I do people getting suspicious of us buying a lot of sugar and cracked corn."

"I thought you were comfortable with telling people that the sugar was for making chokecherry preserves and syrup and the corn is for my chickens."

"I am, I am it's just sometimes -." Phil paused suddenly and looked away. He sighed deeply causing his chest to rise and fall and then he came back to her. "We've got to put the fear of getting caught out of our minds, if we don't we'll never be able to see this through. For me, that might be easier as I don't have much choice. But you, yer educated. You've got a job."

Catarina came back quick, surprising Phil. "This is the only way I'll be able to save my homestead, to have land of my own."

Phil thought, *I wish Martha would've been that committed to our farm.* He said aloud, "Well then, we're gonna do this?"

"Yes, I'm sorry. I didn't mean to waiver."

Phil smiled. "All right, let's go get our supplies."

They parked in front of the Baker Mercantile. It was a big white clapboard building with a false front that made it look larger than it really was. Bold black letters, fat and wide and tall had been painted across the top of this façade to identify what was inside. There was just about everything a home-steader would need. The proprietor, old Ned Peterson, did not question their purchase of 100 pounds of sugar or 300 pounds of cracked corn. But when Catarina laid extra yeast on the counter he came back while looking at Phil, "Looks like someone is going to be getting some homemade bread. I'll bet its real good comin' from yer oven Miss Maricelli."

Phil's paranoia instantly kicked in causing him to think, *Why you old turd.*

Catarina came back. "The times are so uncertain, I'm stocking up while I've got a few dollars."

Ned Peterson, oblivious as to how he'd been taken, moved on. "Well, that's smart thinkin' Miss Maricelli. There's too many people that don't plan ahead." He paused and added the yeast to her ticket. "Will there be anything else?"

"Yes, I need three, ten gallon milk cans."

Knowing that Catarina didn't have dairy cows, Peterson looked at her to be sure that he'd heard right. He repeated, "You want three ah those?"

Phil's heart suddenly began to race. *Dammit, I knew we were getting too much of what we need here.* Two of the cans would be for blending the mash and the other would be for cooking it down and taking the alcohol off.

Catarina's voice failed her at first and then she cleared her throat. "Yes, I haul water from my spring down to the house. These cans will give me more storage."

Suddenly, it made perfect sense to Peterson. "Oh, all right, I'll go get those. They're out back. It'll be just a minute."

Peterson disappeared from behind the counter down a hallway lined with shelves of goods and through a door that led outside to a fenced yard where he kept large items such as milk cans. The door to the yard had no sooner closed when a middle aged man with dark hair and moustache who had been within earshot looking at gloves suddenly walked over. He said, kind of smart-alecky in a low tone, "I got some copper tubin' I'll sell ya cheap." And then he laughed just briefly.

Phil and Catarina feigned ignorance. Phil came back. "I'm sorry Mister, but I don't have any use for copper tubing."

The stranger was about Phil's size. He was dressed in Levis with the cuffs rolled up about two inches, logger type boots, a gray cotton shirt and a flat cloth cap with a short bill.

He smiled in a coy way. "My mistake, I just saw you and your lady friend had purchased all the makin's for corn liquor and well – I guess my imagination just got the better of me."

"Just a coincidence, I guess."

The stranger laughed again. "Good thing I'm not the law."

"It wouldn't matter to us if you were."

"Oh, I'm sure it wouldn't. Besides you two just don't look like you'd be the type to make shine."

"What type would that be?"

"Well, ya gotta know what yer doin'."

"So we look stupid to ya?"

"I ain't sayin' that but bad shine has been known to kill people or make 'em go blind."

"I've heard that."

"Well, you know then if your shine kills somebody the Feds can come back on you? It ain't no simple hillbilly process. "

It was playing in Phil's mind what Jack had said about Siegler's expertise in making moonshine. He'd not taken it very seriously at the time as he just didn't like the man, but now he wondered if he wasn't getting in over his head. He glanced at Catarina. Fear and doubt had returned to her face. He absorbed this before turning back to the stranger. "Soon as we're done, I'll stand ya to a cup of coffee at the café two doors down from here, that is if yer ah mind to?"

The stranger smiled in a respectful way. "I'll meet ya there."

They'd barely concluded their conversation when the back door to the store opened and Ned Peterson came in with the milk cans and began banging and clanging his way up the narrow hallway towards the counter. His demeanor gave no hint that he thought their purchases were intended for anything of a nefarious nature. The stranger, on the other hand, had given life to the paranoia that they had cast aside on the way to town. It wasn't until the truck was loaded and old man Peterson had gone back inside that they were able to purge their minds.

Catarina looked around and then back at Phil. She spit her words out like they tasted bad. "Why are you doing this?"

"He's already on to us."

"That's no reason to let him know anything more."

"He sounds as if he could be helpful."

Catarina's eyes telegraphed her disbelief. "I thought you knew what you were doing."

"I did too until this fella started goin' on about bad shine killin' folks."

"So you don't know how to make it?"

Phil sighed and briefly looked away having withered under Catarina's hostile stare. He came back. "I've never made shine before. But I'm sure I can get on to the process if I have some pointers."

Catarina scoffed and rolled her eyes before, once again, locking them onto Phil. "You need to be schooled in this matter is what you're saying?"

Phil imagined himself as one of her students and she was berating him. It was causing his anger to grow, but he told himself to keep it inside so as to not jeopardize things between them. Still, it was an effort to not flavor his words with it. "I'm sorry. I guess I shudda been more forthright with you. I know the basic process ah makin' shine, it's just some of the finer points, the stuff that might kill a person that I'm not certain of."

Catarina went silent, searching Phil's face for some sign of confidence in what they were about to do. She went on for a time, her anger appearing to be draining away until at last it was gone. She sighed. "All right, let's go talk to this man."

Phil nodded. They began walking side by side towards the café. The impulse to take hold of Catarina's hand, as he would have Martha's, flashed through Phil's mind. He missed that closeness.

Phil opened the door to the Owl Café and allowed Catarina to go in first. It was a small place. A lunch counter made of a hardwood that had been smoothed and polished dominated the left side of the room. Four round-topped wooden stools that were coated with a dark stain sat in front of it. At the moment, all of them were empty. Beyond the counter was an order-up window through which part of the kitchen and a gray haired unshaven man was visible. Beneath the window was another lower counter that held glasses and cups and pies and cake. On the right side of the room were five wooden tables with chairs. Oilcloth that had yellow flowers on a white background covered the tops of the tables. It appeared dingy and well-worn and was not out of character with the scarred and faded green linoleum floor, but it did nothing to lessen the undignified ending of the buck deer whose head hung on the wall opposite the front door. Of the five tables, three were occupied, two by strangers and the last by Phil and Catarina's new acquaintance who had taken a seat at the far end of the room. As they neared his table he stood up and extended his hand to Phil. "Name's Roy Mcleod."

Phil was slightly taken aback as he wasn't certain that he wanted the man to know his name but then it flashed in his mind; *well shit, I've put my foot in it now*. He shook the man's hand. "Phil Caldwell. This is my friend Miss Maricelli."

Mcleod nodded toward Catarina and then shifted his attention to Phil. "Have a chair."

Phil pulled out Catarina's chair for her while Mcleod, who had already sat down, watched as if it was something odd. There was an awkward tension in the air that was suddenly broken by the arrival of the waitress, a frumpy middle aged woman with blonde hair. Her expression suggested she was angry with life. "What can I git for you folks?"

"Just coffee," said Phil.

Catarina looked at the woman. "Yes, just coffee."

The waitress shifted her attention to Mcleod. "And what about you, Roy? You gonna eat?"

"No Bernice, I believe coffee will do me as well."

Disgust came to her face. She scoffed. "You know we're gonna haf ta close this joint if people don't start eatin' somethin'."

"All right, bring me a cinnamon roll."

"You want some melted butter on it?"

"Yeah, that sounds good."

Bernice flashed a look of indifference at Phil and Catarina and then walked away favoring her right leg.

Phil grinned toward Mcleod almost like they were friends. "If I'd known the help here had the temperament of ah grizzly bear I wudda suggested someplace else."

Mcleod laughed politely. "Bernice is ok. Her husband is the cook. They're just tryin' ta make ah livin' in these times when everything in life seems to be contrary to that happenin'."

"So you're a regular here?"

"Used to be before I went to Denver."

"What took ya there?"

Mcleod smiled and lowered his voice. "Business."

Phil could see that Catarina was uneasy, almost like she was in the presence of evil. But they had come, knowing full well how it might be. He went on. "I take it you have concluded your dealings there."

"Not entirely. They were interrupted."

"How's that?"

"I was un-expectantly made a guest of the State of Colorado for damned near a year."

Phil could see that Bernice was coming with their coffee and Mcleod's roll. He came back with, "It certainly has been hot lately."

Bernice set the coffee and roll on the table. "Need anything else?"

Mcleod shook his head. "No Ma'am, I believe this will do us for now."

Bernice was barely out of hearing when Mcleod cut to it. "There's opportunity in Denver but John Law sleeps with my picture on his night stand so I can't go, but I know people there who would buy all the product we can make."

Mcleod had suddenly leapt to a place that Phil had feared all along he was going to. Phil seized on what troubled him most. "We? Ain't you gittin' ah little ahead yerself?"

A derisive smile came to Mcleod's face as he leaned across the table towards Phil. "Let me give you some advice. You two pilgrims deliver some bad product to a customer that's countin' on it for his business and it might not bode well for you."

Catarina came to life, taking Mcleod by surprise. She looked him straight in the eyes. Her words were sharp, almost like they had popped from the end of a bullwhip. "You're an arrogant ass Mr. Mcleod and we are not going to allow you to bully your way into our affairs." And then she looked at Phil. "Maybe we should go."

"My apologies Ma'am. I didn't mean ta talk down to ya, it's just that I'm experienced in these matters and I believe I can be of some help to you."

Catarina started to slide her chair back when Phil spoke up. "Maybe he can be of help."

"He looks upon us as a couple of hayseed fools."

Phil shrugged. "Maybe so, but any agreement would be on our terms as I believe his history with the authorities makes him a liability as much as it does an asset."

Mcleod came back. "It's an art to distill good liquor and I promise you I can do that. A person has got to be able to separate his heads and tails from his hearts and know enough to only keep the hearts. You got to be able to regulate your heat right. Ain't everbody can do it, but I can. "

Catarina looked annoyed, like Mcleod was purposely trying to snowball them with foreign terms. Phil looked at her. "It's not beyond us to learn this, but if we had someone experienced it might help us reach our goals so we can quit all this nonsense."

Catarina sighed. "Do you understand all of this heads and tails stuff?"

"Enough to know that there is truth in what he's saying."

And then it was almost simultaneous, the door opening and an older gray haired man entering the café quick like, as if he was on a mission of some sort and calling out to Bernice as he headed for one of the counter stools; "Did ya hear? Ole Pete Orosco and one ah his hands blew themselves up last night? The Sheriff and the coroner just got back from there."

Bernice was coming from behind the counter with the coffee pot. She stopped all of a sudden and focused on the old man. "Well, how'd they git blown up?"

The old man grinned. "Wiley said their still blew up on 'em. Burned their barn down with them in it."

"The hell you say. Pete Orosco making moonshine with all the land and cattle he's got, why would he want to do such a thing?"

The old man laughed as if Orosco's death meant nothing to him. "I don't know but the damned fool ain't gonna be doin' it anymore." And then he laughed again but he was alone in this.

Mcleod caught Phil's eye. "Like I said, a man's got ta know what he's doin'. If ya don't kill somebody else you could kill yerself."

Phil thought back to that day when he and Jack had been in the barn and the odor of alcohol hung so heavy in the air. It was easy to imagine how the place might blow up if someone were to light a cigarette. However, as much as he disliked Orosco and Siegler, he couldn't envision either one of them or for that matter anyone, working around a still indoors being that stupid. Nonetheless, he allowed Mcleod's banter to go unchecked. "Yeah, that's ah helluva deal those fellas blowin' their selves up."

The passing of Orosco and Siegler began its slide into obscurity as Mcleod moved on. "So do we have deal?"

Phil looked at Catarina. There was nothing comfortable about her demeanor but he asked anyway. "Whaddaya think?"

She made no attempt to hide her anger. "I think we've lost control of things. This started out as simple, almost innocent, and now it strikes me as dirty and vulgar. People being killed or going to jail. I don't know that I want any part of it."

Mcleod went out of turn. "Ma'am, ya just gotta be smart about this and you'll be ok."

Catarina glared at him. "Says the man who just got out of the Colorado penitentiary."

Phil shot an angry look at Mcleod before coming back to Catarina. "We'll do just what we said. We won't be greedy, just enough to pay our bills and git us through to the next plantin' season." He paused in the midst of her silence, and then he added, "I got no choice."

Catarina pursed her lips tightly and shook her head as if she was greatly conflicted or in pain. "All right, but we do this like we had planned. Mr. Mcleod is not in charge."

Mcleod cut in. "This is your parade Ma'am. I'm just tagging along, but I do expect an equal share of the profits. After all, I'm supplying the know-how to make the stuff and I can point ya to some good places to sell your product."

Phil raised his hand so as to disrupt Mcleod's view of Catarina. "You git 20 percent and nothing more."

"My truck's already set up to haul a hunderd gallons. I suspect yers isn't."

Phil instantly did the math of $17 times 100 gallons. Three trips and he and Catarina's money problems would be solved and he could help Jack too. Nonetheless he came back. "I can just as easy set mine up that way. I've seen a truck that's been outfitted like that."

Mcleod smiled as if he and Phil were playing chess and he was about to declare checkmate. "You bought a lot of corn and sugar today. But, the hard cold facts of the matter is that ain't gonna be nearly enough to brew the amount of product you two seem to be wantin'. So you come waltzin' back here to git more and guess what? I suspect old man Peterson would feel obligated to let the sheriff know of yer purchases. But I know folks that'll sell you all the corn and sugar you want and keep their mouths shut. So, I'm thinkin' my participation in this venture is worth a third."

Phil knew Mcleod had a good case for being an equal partner. He was, quite possibly, bringing those things that would make the operation a success as opposed to him and Catarina muddling through it. Still, thirty minutes ago he didn't know this ex con and now here he was making plans to break the law with him. And then his disbelief went back to a month ago when the making of moonshine, going to jail, Orosco and Martha being dead, none of it had a place even in his wildest thoughts. *How in the hell did I git here?* He felt as if he was a stranger to himself. Both Catarina and Mcleod were waiting on his response. Finally, he emerged from his thoughts. "Come Thanksgiving, I want this whole affair to be a distant memory. So Mcleod," Phil hesitated briefly and glanced over at Catarina as if to forewarn her of what he was about to say before going on, "if you can make that happen you can have a third as far as I'm concerned."

Catarina huffed in a defiant, forceful way and tossed her head back slightly but said nothing, preferring instead to just glare at Phil.

Mcleod was quick to claim victory. "August is upon us Mr. Caldwell, but I am certain we can meet yer objectives."

"Well, I hope so as I believe the fox who lingers at the hen house will find his self caught."

Mcleod had been primed to continue with his braggadocio, but his recent stint in prison caused him to suddenly rethink his words. He came back more humbly. "I reckon that is sound advice."

CHAPTER FOURTEEN

Perhaps just as critical as all that Roy Mcleod brought to this undertaking was Catarina's image as the wholesome schoolmarm and her spring hidden away amongst the chokecherry bushes in the coulee west of her shack. In a lot of places the bushes were more like trees being twice as high as she was tall. It was more than ample cover to hide a still. However, in spite of these qualities it was proving to be no small task to set up and tend this operation without fear of attracting attention.

Catarina stood in front of her shanty with her hands on her hips. She was wearing men's cotton pants, dark blue in color with riding boots, a white shirt and a gray felt hat to shade her eyes from the sun. Coming up the road in Phil's truck was Phil and Roy Mcleod. They'd been there the day before to take corn, sugar, the milk cans and three 25 gallon steel drums that belonged to Mcleod up to the spring. Already, or so it seemed to Catarina, the tracks leading there were more well defined.

Mcleod was the first to emerge from the truck. "Good morning, Miss Maricelli." His greeting was stilted and intended to mimic her students. He went on. "Are ya'll set to start yer new career as a maker of moonshine?" And then he laughed knowing, but not caring, that he was overbearing and irritating.

Catarina frowned at Mcleod but said nothing before turning toward Phil. "The road Phil, did you notice it? I'm wondering if people won't look at all the use on it and get suspicious. I'm not sure this is such a good idea."

Phil held his emotions in check, Mcleod did not. His mouth dropped open in mock surprise. "Yer ah little late to shut the barn door. The cow's already got out."

Phil looked hard at Mcleod causing the smile on Mcleod's face to vanish like a candle being blown out. He then went on; the tone of his voice was sympathetic. "Like we agreed Catarina, you just tell people that you hired me and Mcleod to build a cistern at yer spring and pipe the water down to yer house. That'd justify there being more use of the road. It makes sense."

It was about half way through what Phil had been saying that Catarina paid him no heed and shifted her focus to a distant cloud of dust and the automobile making it. Her face went from concern when there was doubt, to outright panic when she finally recognized the car as belonging to the Sheriff. Fear caused her voice to quiver but her words, nonetheless, had a bitter smugness to them. "Well, I guess you're going to get a chance to test your belief."

Phil followed Catarina's eyes. He watched, hoping the Sheriff would go on but he did not. He slowed his car in preparation to start up her road and then he did. Phil mumbled. "Well, I'll be go ta hell."

Mcleod was defiant. "We ain't done nuthin' wrong yet. We've got the makings for moonshine but we ain't put it together. And most of all, we ain't got the still up there yet."

Phil looked at Mcleod and laughed derisively. "We've got all the makings for mash," he paused and looked even more intently at Mcleod before adding emphatically, "*and,* we've got three kerosene burners to cook it sittin' right there. So tell me Mcleod, how stupid do you think Wiley Hargis is?" Phil then turned away as the Fallon County Sheriff's car rocked its way through the potholes in Catarina's yard and came to a stop next to his truck. The wind, as it always did in the morning, was coming out of the east. It was gentle, but enough to temporarily envelope the car in its own dust. Catarina's dog Buster, with help from Ranger, greeted the Sheriff as he got out of his car. They were barking excitedly and lunging toward him until Phil hollered out. "Ranger, that's enough. Git over here." Ranger immediately did as he was told and without help, Buster lost interest.

The Sheriff moved on now, unimpeded towards the three of them but his focus was on Phil. He hollered out. "I was comin' ta see ya when I saw yer truck up here."

Phil started for the Sheriff, his mind spinning like a windmill in a hurricane, pumping out possibilities as to why Hargis wanted to see him. Finally, their outstretched hands met and they shook without saying a word as the Sheriff's demeanor was powerfully somber. He said in a low voice. "Maybe we should go for a walk over by the chicken coop. I have some news for you."

Phil did not think his heart could beat any faster than it already was, but he was wrong. Deep down, he suspected why Hargis was there. In the past he'd envisioned this time when he'd find out and what he'd do. It was never good and he'd always hoped that he would be alone, just him and Ranger, but now, things were different somehow. And then suddenly, it was like the voice in his mind took charge and he heard himself say, "No Wiley, just tell it to me here."

They were within earshot of Catarina and Mcleod. There were no other sounds to interfere with their hearing save for an occasional chicken clucking as it searched the ground for insects and a meadowlark off in the distance. Nonetheless, their morbid curiosity had paralyzed them. Not even a frown from Wiley could shame them away. He sighed and then went to it. "Those FBI boys that was here back when all this business with Martha took place told me about a blood test they got. They call it the Uhlenhuth. Supposedly, it can tell what species a particular blood sample comes from."

"Species? Whaddaya mean?"

Wiley shook his head and sighed. His voice was hesitant. "Well, I just got the results back from those FBI boys in Chicago. I ain't exactly certain why somebody would do this but the blood on Martha's bonnet came from a chicken."

"Ah chicken? Why in the hell would somebody put chicken blood on Martha's bonnet and leave it so I'd find it?" Phil stared at the Sheriff as if he expected an answer that made sense, something that could compete with the painful thoughts that were coming to his mind.

Finally, Wiley gave in to Phil's hostile gaze. "It seems mean spirited to me but it suggests she might be alive."

Phil shook his head as if he were in pain. He had tears in his eyes now and he regretted not taking the walk. "But why Sheriff? It's like it wasn't enough that they take Martha away. They wanted me to believe that she was dead and that she'd likely been beaten to death. Takes a cruel person ta do somethin' like that."

Wiley shook his head. "People like that got twisted thinkin'. There's no figurin' em out but for some reason they wanted ta hurt ya bad. It's like they wanted ta take away yer hope of Martha ever comin' back."

Phil turned away from all of them and looked out over Catarina's wheat field that had been decimated by the hail. He allowed the tears to stream silently down his cheeks. *Never shudda come to this damned country. Been nuthin' but heartache.*

Wiley edged into Phil's thoughts. "Is there anyone you can think of that might want ta hurt you this bad?"

Phil kept his back to the Sheriff. He shook his head. "Hell, I don't know that many people here. There ain't but a handful that live clear out here and we seldom went ta town so who am I gonna piss off?"

In a way Phil had possibly answered the Sheriff's question but, at this very moment, it would have been as cruel as the man who took Martha to point it out. Wiley stepped closer and put his hand on Phil's shoulder. He'd said it in the past, but today was like resurrecting old pain so he said it again. "I'm sorry for yer loss."

Phil wiped at his cheeks and the snot that had run into his moustache before turning around. He came back. "So, is this the end of it?"

"No, but the trail has gotten mighty cold."

"I'm certain the fella who took Martha escaped this country by way of Pete Orosco's."

"I'd thought ah that but Orosco keeps the gates to his ranch locked. If somebody was ta go that way it would've been with Orosco's knowledge and ain't nobody gonna be tappin' in ta that now."

It occurred to Phil to tell the Sheriff that he'd asked Orosco about the stranger coming through his land and that he was certain that Orosco was lying to him. But he kept quiet out of fear that he would incriminate his self and jeopardize what they were presently doing.

Wiley put his hands on his hips, his right nestled just above the grip of his Colt .38 which rode high, and looked Phil in the eyes like he had something important to say. "I know what some people say about me but you should know, I'm like ah dog with ah bone in matters such as this. It may take some time but I'll git you satisfaction."

There was no disguising his emotions of just a moment ago but Phil's anger had caused his eyes and nose to dry up and his voice to become more steady. And then his bravado spilled over like a kettle of boiling water. "I'll tell ya Sheriff, I hope you catch up to this fella before I do as I'm of a mind ta kill the sonovabitch."

Wiley came back quick. "You don't wanna go there. And I don't think I need ta tell ya why, do I?"

There was no getting back at the stranger. For an instant, it had felt good to Phil to spew that vile epithet regardless of how hollow it might have been. But the Sheriff had deprived him of that. There was no place for his anger to go. "Dammit Sheriff, this fella has wronged me. This is man ta man. This is somethin' the law can't satisfy."

"That's foolish talk, Phil. I don't wanna hear any more of it. There'll be nuthin' but trouble come yer way if you continue with that kind of thinkin'.

From the corner of his eye Phil could see Catarina and Mcleod. Their expressions, Catarina's more so than Mcleod's, conveyed clearly what the Sheriff was trying to convince him of. Catarina looked as if she no longer knew the man she once considered a friend. It was this image that brought Phil to his senses. He sighed deeply, reining in the tone of his voice to where it was mostly calm but with a slight edge to it, so as to make his point. "Wiley, ya come here with news that's akin ta pokin' me in the eye with a sharp stick and ya expect me ta not git mad, ta not holler out. It ain't natural for ah man ta not do that."

The Sheriff studied Phil's eyes for a moment and then came back with a hint of compassion but no nonsense. "I'll give ya ta-day, but from here on ya gotta do away with all this killin' talk. Alright?"

Phil nodded. "You'll let me know if you hear of anything else?"

"I will, I surely will."

Wiley turned away and began walking towards his car like he had just finished making a house of cards and he wanted to get away from it before it collapsed. Phil trailed after him. At his car, Wiley purposely gave Mcleod a long look that was bordering on a stare before asking like it was his business, "What ya'll doin'?"

"I've hired these gentlemen to build me a cement cistern at my spring and pipe the water down to my house."

Wiley shifted his attention to Catarina. "That'll be real nice, Ma'am."

"It truly will. It'll be quite the luxury way out here in my little shack."

Wiley appeared almost uneasy like he had something else to say. He made a half turn so his eyes could better sweep over Catarina's yard, beginning with Mcleod and ending at Phil's truck. It was fortunate there were bags of cement on it. He smiled and opened the door of his car before hollering out, "Well, I don't envy you shoveling cement under this hot sun."

Mcleod came back. "We can probably find ah shovel that'll fit yer hands even as soft as they no doubt are."

Phil cringed. He tried to not look at Mcleod too hard lest he giveaway his thoughts. *Why you dumb sonovabitch.*

And then Wiley laughed. "Naw, I doubt it. Since I got this sheriff job I've found manual labor disagrees with me."

And then he laughed again as did Phil and Catarina whereas Mcleod appeared miffed that he'd been one-upped. Wiley started his car and headed back towards the main road.

As Phil began walking toward where Catarina and Mcleod were standing his intention was to chastise Mcleod for being disrespectful to the Sheriff and drawing more attention to himself and to them, but by the time he got there he'd abandoned that idea. *Ain't no changin' that guy. Common sense and his brain ain't ah good fit.*

Catarina was first to address his newly acquired grief. "Maybe there's reason to hope that Martha's alive."

"It's ah mean trick that this fella has played upon me. You'd think he'd be satisfied with takin' Martha but ta make me think he'd beat her head in is – I just don't understand that kind of wickedness, do you?"

"No, I can't explain it but throughout time there's always been people like that, just full of evil. Hopefully, in the end they'll get what's do them."

Mcleod jumped in, seemingly indifferent to Phil's anguish. "I'm gonna head up to the spring. Start mixin' some mash."

Phil glared at Mcleod. Undeterred, he came back. "Takes ten days maybe two weeks before the mash'll be ready to run through the still." He paused and then added as if Phil needed to be reminded. "We ain't gonna make any money 'til we got some product ta sell."

Phil's anger flared but he didn't allow it to escape. *And the sooner we sell some product the sooner we can go our separate ways.* He said aloud. "We'll drive up in the truck."

Catarina caught Phil's eye. "I'll be along shortly. I was about to put a pie in the oven."

His response was brusque. "Alright."

It was more hurt than insult that registered in Catarina's eyes. Regardless, Phil did not see it. His haste to depart had suddenly become exaggerated. *Alright Mcleod, let's git the hell up there. It ain't you that's lost yer wife.*

They'd ridden about halfway in silence when Mcleod, apparently satisfied that the tension at the house was gone, started in. "We'll start with the milk cans. Each one will need about ten pounds ah corn and about 14 pounds ah sugar. And about four tablespoons of yeast. Then we fill the cans with water and stir it up with ah little heat under it."

At first Phil thought to be mad at Mcleod's indifference to his loss, but then as Mcleod went on the reality of it all struck him. *He knows his business. I don't like'im but he knows how to make this stuff and I don't. The bank'll own me if I can't pull this off.* He came back, trying to sound less than ignorant about the process. "Are you gonna close up the cans?"

Mcleod tried not to gloat in the fact that Phil appeared to have recognized his expertise but he could not suppress a grin. "Not with the lids but we'll tie cheese cloth over the tops. Gotta let that yeast breathe."

Phil nodded. He had heard that others put a tight lid on their mash but who was he to question it. He parked the truck in the bottom of the coulee where the chokecherry bushes petered out. They both got out. It was about 150 yards further up, where the chokecherry bushes were tree-like, that the cistern and moonshine operation would be located. Everything had to be carried up there.

Mcleod looked at the bags of cement on the back of the truck and groaned. "Gonna be a hot sonovabitch today."

Phil pulled a bag of cement off the truck and hefted it onto his right shoulder. He said, as if he had not considered the heat before now, "It appears that way." He did not wait for Mcleod but started off up the footpath. Hard work was his forte.

They had built the forms for the cistern the day before. By the time they got there with the bags of cement they were both sweating profusely, Mcleod more so than Phil, and he was breathing hard and barely able to talk. Phil, on the other hand, was hardly winded. He did not chide Mcleod but allowed him to recover. At last, Mcleod caught his breath. "You ain't normal. You part mule or somethin'."

Phil laughed but just briefly. He'd gained some respect. He came back. "I suppose we otta mix the mash before we work on the cistern."

"I reckon so. Let's git 'er cookin'."

CHAPTER FIFTEEN

In five days they had completed the cistern, piped the water down to Catarina's shanty and started 80 gallons of mash cooking. The first day they had rotated the cans and drums over the kerosene burners. Each burner sat nestled inside a column of rocks that suspended the containers over the flame. At the end of that day, Mcleod had decided that they'd given the mash a good start and that the days were naturally warm enough to keep the fermentation process going, provided they stirred it several times a day.

Catarina had invited Phil and Ranger to supper. His paranoia about appearances had been on the wane until Wiley Hargis had opened the door to the possibility that Martha might not be dead and he wasn't a widower. And then it got aggravated even more now that they were conducting actual moonshine operations. Regardless, he and Ranger walked up and over the ridge so as to not have to park his truck in front of her shack.

Catarina heard Ranger barking at Buster and came outside. She waved at Phil. "That's a good hike."

"Well, I've heard the food is purty good here."

"I hope you like fried chicken."

"I do. Chickens eat real well. Never met one that I didn't like."

Catarina laughed. "Come inside. I've got cold spring water. These gentlemen friends of mine piped it down the coulee for me."

Phil followed after Catarina. The light hearted banter between them felt good. He went on. "Well, look at you. Runnin' water, why next you'll probably be gittin' electricity."

Catarina had already set the table for supper. She picked up their glasses and went to the new spigot protruding from the wall and began filling them. "Go ahead and sit down."

Phil took a seat. He'd felt it before, that woman's touch. Not necessarily the utilitarian things, like the shelves piled high with cans of food and dishes that occupied the wall to either side of the stove and on the wall to his left above the hammered tin sink that they'd put in below the water tap. No, it was the frilly things like the painting of some wildflowers in a mountain meadow on the wall to his right and the white curtains over the window in the front of the shanty that were gathered on each side and tied back with yellow ribbon. It was the canisters for sugar, flour and coffee that were bright blue and labeled with fancy white letters that rested on her counter. Even her bed, off against the wall to the right, with its patchwork quilt of different colored flowers was neatly made. And next to it was a night stand with books and a lantern. Martha had been good at adding a touch like this. And even though he had been to her house numerous times before, it wasn't until tonight that he saw the real Catarina. It gave him a giddy feeling, kind of like when he had first met Martha. And then Catarina, oblivious as to where his mind had taken him, set the glasses of water on the table and announced, "Mcleod came by today and started two more 25 gallon barrels of mash."

Given his mindset of a moment ago, Phil felt a pulse of anger, almost like he'd been trespassed upon. "I didn't know that was his intention."

"He said he just happened upon these barrels and wanted to put them to use."

"I suppose that's good. I just didn't know."

"We're totally out of sugar and low on corn. He wants you to go to Billings to that store he knows of and get more."

Phil scoffed, still smarting from having been left out of the decision to make more mash. "Has he forgot the way to Billings."

Catarina turned away and went to the stove lest her eyes betray her thoughts. She began taking the chicken from a frying pan and placing it on a plate. She said over her shoulder, "I don't know that it is a good idea but he seems to be the one in charge. I'm just doing as he asked."

Phil sighed. They'd become subservient to Mcleod's expertise, his connections, his everything. "I can't git much. I'm nearly broke after paying to git that tank installed in my truck and buying materials for the still."

Catarina set the chicken and some boiled potatoes on the table and sat down. "I would have helped you with that but building the cistern and piping the water cost more than I figured."

Phil laughed in a sarcastic way. "I guess if you have talents like Mcleod you don't need money."

"I'll just be glad when we're done with this. It'd be nice if we could cut our ties with him by Thanksgiving."

"He'll fight us on that."

"Probably so but once we've made what we need I'm through with this and I don't want that still on my land."

Phil reached for a piece of chicken. "It's the first week of August and it'll likely be another week before the mash is ready to run through the still. Thanksgiving may be kind of ambitious."

Catarina spooned some potatoes on to her plate and handed the bowl to Phil. Her expression had suddenly become one of considerable angst, more so than what Mcleod and the moonshine operation might warrant. It was such that Phil purposely caught her eye to verify what he was seeing. She gave in to it. "I received a letter today from the school administration in Baker." She paused as if it was too painful to continue.

A quivery, fearful feeling came over Phil. He softened his voice. "So, what did they say?"

"They're closing the little school here. Too many people have moved away."

"I'm sorry to hear that, Catarina. I truly am."

Her eyes had become watery. "They've got an opening in town. They said I could have it if I want it."

The angst that had been Catarina's alone now permeated Phil's body. He felt weak, almost sick. Six weeks ago, word of the schoolmarm leaving would have meant little to him but not now. His voice was hopeful. "So whaddya yer thoughts on the matter?"

Catarina grimaced and shook her head. "I don't know. I'm torn. I'm close to being able to make application for the patent on my land. I don't want to lose this. It's my home."

Because he did not want her to go Phil was tempted to bolster the false notion that she would lose her homestead if she moved to town, but he did not. "You've done a lot to prove up on yer land. I'm purty certain the government will allow you to be gone part of the year so long as you come back in the summer."

"But who will stir the mash and take care of my chickens?"

"I will."

"People might talk seeing you over here all the time."

Phil laughed. "Hell, the rate farms are goin' under there won't be anybody left to gossip."

Catarina sighed. "I've got a few days to think about it."

"That's probably best. Think on it awhile. No need ta rush a big decision like this."

"No, certainly not."

And then a momentary lull, a silence came over the both of them as they sat there looking across the table at one another. Neither dared speak it but they both shared a contempt for the ghost, or not, of Martha.

CHAPTER SIXTEEN

On the morning after the evening he had supper with Catarina, Phil started out for the Rosebud Mercantile in Billings. It would be an all day trip as the roads were rough and slow going, especially from Baker to Miles City. However, from Miles City on the road improved and since it followed the Yellowstone River all the way to Billings it gave the illusion, so long as you were looking that direction, that the land was more lush and forgiving and not being crippled by drought. But if you looked away from the river, it was an endless milieu of coulees and mesas covered with yellow grass, sage and scattered juniper trees. As he drove along, Phil couldn't help but envision General Custer and his men in the midst of this bleakness trying to find their way. He wondered too if the men realized that Custer was a reckless, egotistical fool. And then, since he had time on his hands, he speculated what he would do if he had been a lowly private, or for that matter, anyone of a lesser rank under Custer. It came to him. *Somebody shudda shot that sonovabitch and saved all those lives.* He couldn't put the suffering of the horses and men and finally their deaths out of mind until about four o'clock when he arrived in Billings. A good room and a good meal were not within his budget so he opted to check into a fleabag hotel and have a steak for supper. The hotel clerk had recommended the Rimrock Café, a few blocks down the street as the place to go. In spite of it being hot, the walk went quickly and Phil soon found himself in front of a lightweight wooden door whose top half was a fine screen. As he pulled the door open a long coiled spring attached to it resisted his efforts and banged it shut behind him.

A young woman, maybe 30 with blonde hair and a slender build wearing a pinkish skirt that came down to her shins with a white blouse called out to him as she whisked by. "Sit where you want."

It was an old building whose walls looked like a stone aggregate of various sizes, shapes and colors. The floors, on the other hand, were a dark wood and reflected lots of use. The room had a high ceiling. Suspended from it was a fan whose blades wobbled and spun endlessly. Down the center of the room, protruding from metal pipes hanging from the ceiling were frosted white orbs containing gas lights. They had not yet been turned on. At the far end of the room was the kitchen. In front of it was a counter that was accompanied by five round seats mounted atop shiny metal posts that were bolted to the floor. The covers of the seats were red and appeared to be hard and slick. A man, who was grossly obese, sat on the center stool. The cheeks of his butt had enveloped its top to the point it looked like he was sitting only on the shiny metal post. There were booths with high backed wooden bench seats along the walls and tables and chairs in the center of the floor. One of the tables and one of the booths were occupied. Phil slid into a booth out of view of the big man with the shiny post up his butt. Seconds later, the blonde girl reappeared and dropped a menu in front of him. "What can I get you to drink?"

"Water, cold water."

The waitress raised her ticket pad and wrote the water down. And then she looked Phil over for a few seconds and came back. "I can get you something stronger if you like."

"Stronger?"

The girl nodded over her shoulder to a closed door just beyond Phil's booth. "They've got spirits in the billiards room."

Phil smiled. "You must have an understanding police force."

"I guess as long as no trouble comes of it, they'll allow it."

"Well, maybe later. Right now I'm in need of a good T-bone steak and some fried spuds and biscuits and corn on the cob."

The girl began to write again. "How do you want your steak cooked?"

"Medium well."

"You sure I can't get you something from the billiards room?"

Phil looked at the waitress as if to question her persistence. She appeared disappointed. He wondered if she got a commission on drinks. Nonetheless, he came back. "I'm good. I generally don't care to mix spirits with my food."

She started to frown but caught herself and took the menu back. "I'll get your water."

Phil watched as the girl walked off. She was shapely and pretty in kind of a plain sort of way. *I bet she sells plenty ah drinks ta fellas, especially single ones.* And then he suddenly felt sad. It was like somebody had flipped a switch. He could hear Catarina telling him when he got back that she was going to live in Baker. He sighed. *What am I doing? I might still have a wife.* He could hear the cook's radio playing in the kitchen. It took him to a restaurant in Lincoln that played a radio. It had been Martha's favorite place to eat. When they could afford it, they would go there in the evenings and she would laugh sometimes till she cried at the Amos and Andy show. And then there was the music of Guy Lombardo and the Canadians. Life had been good until he had insisted they come to Montana and homestead where there was no electricity and no radio. He sighed heavily as he reached into his shirt pocket for his Lucky Strikes and matches. *Now look at us. Been close to a month and I don't even know for sure what's happened to her.* He struck a match and lit his cigarette. His face was shrouded in smoke when the blonde girl returned.

"Here's your water."

He caught her eye. "You know, I've changed my mind. I believe I'll have ah coupla fingers of sippin' whiskey."

Her dour look instantly went away. "I'll be right back."

The door to the billiards room was dark and heavy with a big brass handle, the kind with the thumb lever you pressed down. As the door swung open bits of conversation escaped like birds from a cage. "Ah man can't drill too many dusters or he'll find himself in the poor house. Well, ya damned fool ya just gotta drill in the right spot." And then there was laughter until the door went shut. *Oil people,* thought Phil. His mind drifted. *I don't believe anything ever happened to that oil fella that run the mail man off the road.* He scoffed. *So much for ole Wiley bein' like a dog on ah bone.* From the kitchen, it seemed the radio had gotten louder. The announcer's voice was stern and foreboding. "Investors in Hoover's bull market may one day wish they hadn't been so quick with their dollars. It's a bubble that can't go on as it is." And then the heavy door opened again to the loud pop of a single ivory ball colliding with a triangle assemblage of many ivory balls and a cacophony of voices laced with profanity and laughter and false bravado. For a few seconds it drowned out the radio before the door closed and the girl returned.

"Here's your drink. I'll go check on your steak."

Phil nodded. He waited until she had started back to the kitchen before picking up the drink. It was clear like water. According to Mcleod that meant it hadn't been aged in a wooden barrel. But then he had laughed. *What with ever body and their cousin makin' shine the man that takes the time ta age it is gonna lose out.* Phil wondered where the café got their liquor and if he had reason to worry in drinking it. He swirled it in the glass and studied it for impurities. He'd heard those stories of people who left their mash uncovered and mice and insects had drowned in it but they used it anyway. And, as he'd come to understand, it was the moonshine whose maker hadn't boiled off the heads and tails but bottled everything that came out of his still as good product that would kill you or make you go blind. He sighed, still staring at the glass. *What kinda business have I gotten myself into?* And then he took a sip, just enough to challenge his taste buds. It was smooth and did not take his breath away like the shine that Jack had given him.

"Here ya go."

Phil leaned back, allowing the girl room to set the steak and some biscuits down in front of him. Right away he noted a deficiency. "Ya got some butter and preserves to go with them biscuits?"

"Got fresh raspberry jam that folks seem ta really like."

"That'd be just grand."

Phil cut into the steak as the girl went to retrieve the jam and butter. It was tender and cooked to his liking. A Guy Lombardo song had come on the radio causing him to mourn Martha's absence, perhaps more so than at any time since right after it had happened and they had found the bloody bonnet. His mind was awash with nostalgia and sadness as he savored the steak and spuds when all of a sudden a man who had come in off of the street went straight to the billiards room door. He opened it wide and looked inside trying to decide, Phil supposed, if he wanted to go on in. And then one voice rose above the drone of all the others. "You left that poor sonovabitch in the well?" Phil instantly dropped his fork and got to his feet. He edged in beside the stranger holding the door open and looked over the room. It was long and narrow and shrouded in tobacco smoke from its many patrons. Three billiard tables were aligned down its center. To the left of these was a bar with numerous stools in front of it, all of them occupied. On the right side of the room were small round tables and chairs. And then came the voice again, drunk and loud. "I dare say that fella is gonna be hoppin' mad." Phil's eyes locked onto a man standing and leaning back against the bar. He was alternately talking to his friend who was sitting at the bar, and watching the billiards game on the table near them. The man sitting laughed and in that instant it came back to Phil, that laugh and that day. He started toward the men. They were both about his size but he knew that often didn't matter. It was more how a man handled himself and what motivated him. Phil was confident he surpassed them in this regard. He stopped squarely in front of the man sitting on the bar stool. He looked at him in a hateful way. Thinking that Phil was drunk, the man indulged him for a time until finally he said, "Friend, you mind moving along. We're trying to watch the game."

Phil stood still and scoffed. People nearby, sensing trouble, went silent. Phil came back. "You don't know who I am, do you?"

The man appeared slightly fearful. "I'm afraid you've got me there as I don't believe we've ever met."

Phil smiled in an evil, mean way. "I'm the poor sonovabitch you left in the well."

Surprise followed by a flood of fear came to the man's face. It appeared for a moment he was in danger of drowning in it when suddenly he recovered. "I don't know what you're talkin' about."

Phil glanced over at the man standing. "Yer friend here does."

The standing man was quick to come back. "I told'im I thought it was chicken shit ta do what he did."

The man sitting scowled at his friend and then came back to Phil. "Move on Mister. What's done is done. It was all in good fun."

"Fun? I cudda died in that hole."

"But you didn't. So let it go."

No, I been waitin' for this day for a long time. I aim ta give ya a good thrashin' so you can either git yer sorry ass off that stool and take it like a man or I'll commence right now."

A booming voice from behind the bar sounded in the now dead silent room. "There'll be no fightin' in here. You wanna engage in that kinda play take it out back."

Phil looked at the bartender. He had a baseball bat in his hands. It was clear to him there would be no retribution.

"Let me buy you a drink, Mister," said the sitting man. "We'll call it good."

Phil came back in a hateful tone. "I know you now for the despicable coward you are. Don't you ever come on my land again, if you do I promise you it will not bode well for you." And with that, Phil turned and walked out. He was angry and frustrated that he'd gotten no satisfaction after all this time of wondering who had left him to die in the well. It had been a reoccurring fantasy of what he would do, not only to that guy but the one that had taken Martha. But now, here he was even more angry and frustrated. He paused beside his table. At the moment, adrenaline masked his hunger. He was tempted to just pay and go back to his room, but then it came to him. *That sonovabitch wins if I leave this steak sittin' here.* He sat down and right off drank his whiskey in three long swallows. It jolted him hard, distracting him from his anger. He cut a bite of his steak and began to eat, pausing only long enough to gesture with his whiskey glass for the waitress to bring him another one.

It had not been necessary, but Mcleod had cautioned Phil against just waltzing into the Rosebud Mercantile and ordering up 300 pounds each of sugar and corn meal in the presence of other customers. *It'll be a dead giveaway as to what your intentions are and you'll put the proprietor in a bad spot. He'll have ta tell ya no, at least right then and there he will, so you wait until it's just you and him.*

Phil pulled his truck around behind the store. The proprietor, J.B. Tipton helped him load the sugar and corn meal. "That'll be $18.00 for the corn meal and $21.00 for the sugar."

Phil counted out the money. "Here ya go."

Tipton pocketed the cash and looked Phil hard in the eyes. "Just so ya know, if the Feds stop you and ya tell'em where ya got this stuff I'll call ya ah damned liar all day long."

"I wouldn't do that."

"You say that now but just wait till those boys start threatening you with jail or takin' yer truck. Mark my words, they catch you with this much makin's fer mash and they'll be comin' to yer house next."

Phil nodded. He couldn't help but believe that Tipton's words were a prophecy that he was destined to live if he ever came back here again. He tarped the load down to hide it from view and drove around to the front of the store where he pumped 8.5 gallons of gas in his truck and gave Tipton another $2.97. Billings had exacted a heavy price both monetarily and emotionally. He was glad to be leaving but he dreaded the long drive home, mostly because it gave him too much time alone with his thoughts. In his mind it seemed Catarina's going to Baker to teach clouded over most everything else. It made him feel guilty, kind of sick to his stomach to think that he didn't want her to go. *If Martha was ta come home tomorrow, I don't know what I'd do. Maybe it's a good thing, Catarina going ta Baker.*

By the time he got to within sight of her shanty, the sun had moved on to some other part of the world and there were long shadows over the land. In spite of his mixed feelings, he had been all day playing various scenarios in his mind of how it would be when he got to her place. The endless stretch of road along the Yellowstone River had caused him to abandon common sense and morality. But his fantasies were destined to remain in his imagination as Mcleod's truck was parked in front of her shanty. For a moment, he felt entitled to show anger, to be jealous and then he caught himself; *Hell, I'm a married man.* Nonetheless, he felt protective towards her as Mcleod was a coarse man. He parked his truck and got out. Ranger, followed by Buster, came running to greet him. Phil dropped to his knees and allowed Ranger to lick his face. "Oh, I missed you too, Ranger dog. Yes, I did."

"Welcome back."

Phil looked up to see Catarina and Mcleod standing in front of the house.

Mcleod caught his eye. "Did ya git everything?"

"I did, but I ain't got a good feeling about going there again."

"Why's that?"

Phil shrugged. "The Feds ain't so stupid as to be able to find out how much sugar and corn meal the railroad brings to that town and what merchants is gittin' it. Tipton's days are numbered."

"So what do you suggest we do?"

"We make what shine we can from this and call it good."

Mcleod tossed his head back slightly and laughed sarcastically as if to emphasize his disdain for Phil's fear. "We go to all this trouble and yer already wantin' ta quit?"

"I told you we had goals and one of them is to stay out of jail."

"Mine too, but I also want ta make some money."

"As do I, but it's a losing proposition all the way around if the Feds seize our trucks and moonshine and fine us to boot and still send us to jail. I say we don't push our luck."

"I agree," said Catarina. "And the still is on my land. I stand to lose a lot if we're caught."

Mcleod scoffed. "They can't take yer land."

Catarina glared at Mcleod, almost like she was better than him. "I'm a teacher. Going to jail will tarnish my reputation. Parents are not going to want their children being taught by some jail bird booze maker."

Mcleod hesitated as if he knew better, but his growing anger would not allow him to remain quiet. "Well, if yer worried about your reputation I'd say it's a little late for that."

Anger instantly consumed Catarina's face. "What are you talking about?"

"People are already talkin' about how much time you and Mr. Caldwell here are spendin' together."

"There's nothing inappropriate going on. We're just neighbors. And quite frankly, our business arrangement causes us to be together."

Phil jumped in. "Let it go Mcleod. You knew we just wanted to make enough money to git us through to the next planting season."

Mcleod laughed in a mocking way. "You, the master distiller has got that all figured out." He paused and shook his head in disgust. "I'll be back in four days. We'll run our oldest batch of mash then." He laughed again. "You'll see." And with that he got in his truck and drove off.

They stood where they were for a moment, watching Mcleod drive down the coulee towards the main road. Catarina was first to attack the doubt that resided in both their minds. "Do you think he's right?"

"I suspect he is but I couldn't give in to him."

"So what do we do?"

"It's a General Custer thing."

"What?"

"To me the signs are clear, if we git too greedy we'll end up like Custer, or maybe more to the point, like Jack Schneider."

"I agree. We've got to stick together on this."

And then out of the blue Phil went to the other part of what Mcleod had said, not so much out of concern but more he wanted to gauge Catarina's response. "I'm sorry if my being here has caused the gossipers to start up."

She did not shy away from it. "The trail between our places runs both ways."

Her words made him feel good, but at the same time like a scoundrel as well for maneuvering the conversation there, being a married man and all. He went on, emboldened. "What have you decided about going to Baker?"

Catarina sighed. "I'm staying."

For an instant, it flashed in Phil's mind it was because of him. "What about yer job?"

She shook her head. "It's all about appearances, Phil. It might make sense to passers-by if they were to see your truck here each day at about the same time for 15 minutes while you fed my chickens and gathered the eggs. But to see you walking up the coulee to stir the mash three or four times a day would pique people's curiosity, I'm sure. Me, on the other hand, they would assume I was going to pick chokecherries."

"Yer probably right." He paused and frowned. "I'm sorry that I got you bogged down in this mess. You cudda got by without it."

She smiled weakly. "Like I said, the trail runs both ways."

He savored her words for a moment and then came back. "It's close ta dark. I suppose now would be a good time for me to unload this up at the still."

"I'll give you a hand."

"That's alright, I can git it."

"We're business partners, remember?"

A good feeling swept over Phil. It was the first in quite some time. He smiled. "Ok, let's go to it then."

She climbed in the truck with him and they started up the coulee in the fading light with Ranger and Buster trotting behind. They worked well together with her wrestling the sacks to the back of the truck bed and him pulling them off and carrying them up through the trees to the still. The unloading did not take long and they soon found themselves bumping their way back down the coulee towards her shanty. They were just about there when she offered up, "Would you like a sandwich? I've got some canned beef and bread I baked just today."

Phil looked at her. He wondered, or maybe hoped, what her true intentions were. He wanted to accept her hospitality but, once again, the ghost of Martha came to him. He stopped the truck in front of her shanty. "Thanks anyway, but it's been a long day. I believe me and the Ranger dog will just go on home."

Disappointment flickered in her eyes just briefly before she got hold of it and forced a smile. "All right then, you have a good night." She lifted the handle on the door and slid out to the ground and began walking away. He called out. "Goodnight." She kept on walking. He tried to tell himself that she hadn't heard him over the truck's engine, but he knew better.

CHAPTER SEVENTEEN

As he said he would, on the fourth day, Mcleod returned. He arrived at Catarina's shortly before nine o'clock in the morning. Phil, who had walked over the ridge, was inside having coffee and a sweet roll. Ranger, on the other hand, was barking and making false lunges as if he wanted to bite Mcleod causing him to stand still until Phil came outside.

"Call yer damned dog off."

Phil scowled at Mcleod. "Don't you be swearin' at my dog. He's a good judge ah character and he knows sic'em purty good too." And then Phil laughed as did Catarina who had come out now. "That'll do Ranger."

Ranger immediately retreated back to where Phil was standing. He reached down and patted Ranger's head. "Yeah, yer ah good dog."

Mcleod shook his head and began walking towards Phil. "I brought a couple more barrels. I figure with these and what mash we already got cookin' we might end up with 70 or 80 gallons of moonshine."

Phil did a quick calculation in his head. If they priced it at $17 a gallon so as to not be undercut by the Canadian bootleggers they would at most make about $1,200 to $1,400 and that had to be split three ways. However, this was before they deducted their investment in corn meal, sugar, yeast, barrels, modifications to his truck and gas. He knew better but he said it anyway. "That doesn't seem like much. Are you sure about that?"

Mcleod grinned. "Sure enough to bet your homestead on it." He paused and then added, "Yer goal seem ah little outta reach does it?"

Phil sensed it was pointless to argue. He came back in a curt tone, "Maybe we should just run this mash and see what we git. There'll be no guessin' then."

Mcleod looked smug. "No there won't."

Because he had more barrels, Mcleod drove his truck to where they usually parked down from the spring. Phil and Catarina walked up. By the time they got there, Mcleod was busy bucketing mash into the still. "I figure we'll have ta cook three batches to distill what mash we've got ready in the milk cans. It's gonna take some time."

Concern came to Catarina's face. "How long do you figure?"

Mcleod glanced back at her. "Probably three days."

"Three days. That can't be. What will I tell the mail man when he sees your truck parked up here? He'll ask. I've already explained to him how you and Phil built the cistern and piped water to my house. I don't know what to tell him now."

Mcleod set the bucket down and faced Catarina. "You tell'im that you had a leaky pipe and that I brought a new joint out from town and replaced it."

"That may do for today but what about the two days after that?"

For a moment Mcleod was mute and then he came back. "Well, I reckon you two are gonna have to learn how to cook down mash."

Catarina looked to Phil. "I don't know. I don't want to kill somebody with this stuff."

"Neither do I but I'm not certain how we would explain Mcleod's truck being at either one of our places for three days. People would question it and those that know of his past would draw their conclusions purty quick I suspect, and it wouldn't be any time at all before they would be tattlin' to the sheriff. I just don't know that we got much choice."

And then Mcleod laughed in a way that suggested it was a precursor to some sort of vulgarity. He glanced over at Phil before quickly settling his eyes on Catarina. "You could just tell folks that I'm your man friend and I've come to stay."

Anger instantly overtook her. "That will never happen, Mr. Mcleod. I'd rather risk going to jail and damaging my reputation in that manner than have people think I was sleeping with you."

Mcleod recoiled like Catarina had spit in his face. "Yer ah little late ta salvage your reputation, Miss Maricelli. You and Caldwell ain't foolin' nobody. So you might as well git off yer high horse."

Phil stepped towards Mcleod, his right hand clenched into a fist. "Shut your filthy mouth."

Mcleod laughed. "Go ahead and hit me. See how much shine you two fools git made then."

"He's right, Phil. Let it go. We're too far into this to throw it all away now."

Phil continued to stare at Mcleod until the smug look on his face had melted. Mcleod came back, in a respectful tone, "My apologies, Miss Maricelli."

An awkward silence overcame them as Catarina gauged Mcleod's sincerity until finally she said, "I accept your apology."

Phil remained in a confrontational stance near Mcleod. Catarina came back, in a louder, agitated voice, "It's ok, Phil.

Let's just get on with this. The quicker we do the sooner we can be shed of wondering what people will think."

For a brief moment, it appeared Catarina's words would have no effect on Phil but then he sighed deeply. "All right but there can't be a repeat of what just took place here, if there is I'm of the opinion our partnership will be done in. Do you agree Mcleod?"

Mcleod nodded. "Yeah, I'm regretting having ever tied up with you two so, yeah, let's git on with it." And with that he picked up the bucket and began filling it with fermented mash and dumping it into the big copper pot at the base of the still. He said, in an almost conciliatory voice, "You wanna light the burner?"

Phil dropped to his knees beside the 20 gallon copper pot and fired up the kerosene burner beneath it.

"A moderate flame will do to start with," added Mcleod. "We'll cook off the heads or bad alcohol first. You'll know it by its sweet smell and the fact that it burns all the way down if ya drink it." And then he turned to Catarina. "Put one of them quart jars under the end of the coil. We'll probably come close ta fillin' that and tossin' it 'fore we git into the hearts or the stuff we'll keep."

Catarina took a Mason jar from a cardboard box and placed it as Mcleod had asked.

He caught her eye. "It'll likely be an hour before this comes to a boil."

"So what do we do in the meantime?"

"Watch it. Think ah all the money yer gonna make."

Catarina, more at ease now, laughed. "This kind of reminds me of baking pies. You do all this blending of in-gredients and then put it in the oven and wait to take it out."

Still on his knees, Phil felt of the big copper kettle. It was cool to the touch. "Well it's gonna be a good while before this pie is done."

"We don't wanna rush things," said Mcleod. "We need ta let the heads run their course 'fore we crank up the heat."

It was a good hour, just as Mcleod had predicted, before the mash inside the still began to boil. Phil, who had been sitting next to Catarina on a big rock nearby, could hear it. He too had been taken with a resigned comradery. Nobody talked of the angry words they'd had earlier. It was like they were content to let them die for the common good. His tone reflected that feeling. "She's ah percolatin' now."

From the other side of the still where he was sitting cross-legged on the ground, Mcleod came back, "Keep ah close eye on 'er. When she starts makin' product toggle yer flame down to where there's about 8 to 12 drips per second. After that dries up, we'll be ready to increase the heat and collect the good stuff."

"So, where'd you learn all this?"

Mcleod had a piece of grass about six inches long hanging from the right side of his mouth. It bobbed up and down as he spoke. "My family's from Tennessee. Making moonshine goes way back but I guess it was my uncle on my ma's side that really educated me on the matter."

"I didn't realize there was so much to it."

"Well, you need ta pay close attention cuz after today it'll be up ta you and Miss Maricelli to git it right. If we put out some bad product we could have more 'n the law come lookin' for us."

At that moment it occurred to Phil that his life would have been a lot simpler if things had worked out with Orosco. He briefly teased this thought before coming back to where he was. "I kinda figured that. All I can say is, we'll do our best."

Catarina blurted out in an excited voice. "It's starting."

Mcleod came back. "Let 'er git rollin' and then count the drops and adjust yer heat accordingly."

Phil focused on the end of the coil and tried counting the drops in a second. It soon became apparent to him that it was next to impossible to distinguish individual drops within a second, at least 8 to 12 of them it was. "There ain't no way in hell that I can make out drops. It's comin' too fast."

"All right then, turn yer heat down."

Phil did as Mcleod ordered and then the three of them watched as the Mason jar slowly filled. They sat swatting at deer flies, wiping beads of sweat from their faces and saying little to one another. From time to time a gentle breeze would rustle the leaves of the chokecherry bushes and caress their faces with cool air, but it was short lived. Catarina broke the monotony of watching the bad stuff go into the jar. "I believe in my prayers tonight, I'm going to ask God to eliminate deer flies from the earth or, if he's not inclined to do that, just this coulee."

Phil obliged her with a short laugh but it was Mcleod who ruined the moment. "Maybe it was God who sent those deer flies to dissuade us from our evil undertaking."

Phil looked at Mcleod and then Catarina. The smile that had come to her face suddenly went away. He was of a mind to say something but he did not.

Mcleod came again. "She's slowed way up. Won't be long now." He waited for an acknowledgement from Phil or Catarina but they acted as if they hadn't heard him. In about ten minutes the bad stuff or the 'Heads' were done. It had taken two hours to get to this point.

Phil got up and started for the burner beneath the still. "So how hot do I make it?"

"Just nudge it up a little and then give it a few minutes. Put a clean jar under the coil too. Now we'll collect the 'Hearts', the good stuff."

Phil looked at the quart jar and then it came to him how far he and Catarina were from realizing their goal. It was humbling, if not aggravating, knowing that Mcleod was right. It wasn't long, however, before the good stuff began to drip, tortuously slow, one quart jar at a time. And so on they went throughout the day and into early evening capturing the 'product' that would save their homesteads and Mcleod from having to find work where there was little to be had. It was around seven o'clock when Phil, who was sitting Indian style on the ground near the collecting jar, alerted Mcleod. "It's startin' to stink like a wet dog. Just like you said it would. Whaddaya want me ta do?"

The collection jar was close to being full. "Pull that jar out. We'll save it. From here on we'll be in the 'Tails' and we'll not keep it. In fact, you can turn the burner off."

Catarina took the near full jar from Phil and handed him an empty one to catch what tails would come off before the still cooled. She then poured the 'good stuff' into a 20 gallon wooden keg that Mcleod had brought. It was the 16th jar or four gallons from the first batch of mash that had been in one of the ten gallon milk cans. The relatively meager amount for the three of them to have gotten for their day long efforts was not lost on her. Mcleod noted the look on her face. "It don't look like much cuz it ain't."

Catarina studied Mcleod. He was not outwardly gloating but close to it. She indulged him. "Maybe we will have to purchase more supplies."

Phil cut in, surprised at her sudden change of heart. "With what, Catarina? I'm broke. Besides we're gonna git ourselves caught if we keep goin' ta town and buyin the makin's fer mash."

Catarina appeared to regret her words. "I'm sorry, it's just – well, look at this. We've been here all day for this? It's a slap in the face."

Phil sighed and shook his head. "Maybe we can talk later but for now we've got plenty of mash to process. At this rate, it's gonna take a long time."

"And don't forget," said Mcleod, "ya need ta clean the still before you run another batch. It'll be dark soon so you may want to not wait too long before you do that."

"Yer leavin'?"

"It's a long ways back ta town. I don't wanna drive it in the dark if I can help it. Damned badgers have dug holes in a coupla places that'll loose yer fillin's if ya hit'em square on."

Phil suppressed a frown but couldn't resist making a jab that was poorly disguised as friendly banter. "Well, I guess that's as good of an excuse as any ta git outta cleanin' up."

Mcleod shook his head to the side in an exaggerated manner and then brought his eyes to bear on Phil. "If you feel strongly about it I'll sure as hell stay and lend a hand. We'll just let Miss Maricelli explain to the tongue waggers what my truck was doin' at her place after dark."

Phil hesitated just long enough to let Mcleod know that his words had not set well and then he came back somewhat indifferently. "So when will we see you next?"

"I ain't sure. Might be good if I just stay clear ah here for a while."

"I can't say that I disagree with that notion but it causes me to question what yer role is from here on?"

For a brief moment, Mcleod appeared stumped but then he suddenly came back. "I know where we can sell our product."

Phil scoffed. "So do I. Now that Orosco is out of the picture all of his customers will be needing shine."

"I suspect the Canadian bootleggers have already visited those folks and they've got good product."

"So what's yer grand plan?"

"We go south, way south where the Canadians don't go. We can ask $20 a gallon and git it without a squawk."

"South? Where are you talkin' about?"

"Denver. I know people there. They'll buy all we can make."

Phil laughed derisively. "Aren't you on a first name basis with the law there?"

"It's a big town. I'll blend in."

Phil shook his head. "I don't know. Seems ta me if they spot you, or somebody else that knows you does and they tip off the police, they're gonna want to see what yer up to and if I'm with you we'll both end up in the hoosgow."

The worry in Catarina's eyes over flowed. "I agree with Phil. Denver to me seems risky. Besides, it's a long ways down there and that just makes for more opportunity to be stopped for some random inspection. Once the product leaves here the less time we're in possession of it the better our chances are for not getting caught."

Mcleod came back. "For some reason, I didn't think you'd be goin' on the delivery."

"She's not," said Phil. "She's got ta look after the chickens and the dogs."

Catarina's immediate look suggested she took offense to Phil speaking for her, but then the logic in what he'd said took hold and the edginess left her demeanor causing her to remain silent.

Phil went on. "It's gonna be a good while before we have enough product ready so I reckon we've got time to ponder what we do with it."

"We do," said Mcleod, "but I was thinkin', if we wanna make a trip down to Denver worthwhile we should take at least a hunderd gallons ah shine."

Phil scowled. "I already told you I don't feel good about buyin' more sugar and corn meal. People know plain as day what yer gonna do with it when you buy as much as we do."

"We'll split up the purchases. We'll each go to a different town and buy lesser amounts and make comments about needin' chicken feed and doin' fall canning."

"Ok, and what do we use for money?"

Mcleod glanced down at the keg on the ground. "We sell what we made today and use that money."

Phil looked to Catarina. She gave no indication that, only a moment ago, she'd suggested they buy more supplies. He guessed she'd lost her stomach for it.

"It's a lousy four gallons," said Mcleod. "We can turn that into 30 or 40. Then we'll all have enough to quit this business."

The cautious Catarina returned. "I suspect, Mr. Mcleod, that kind of greedy thinking is what got you and a lot of your fellow inmates a cell in the Colorado penitentiary."

Mcleod appeared perplexed. "There's plenty of people that are making a lot of money from brewin' moonshine who've never seen a day in jail. But these people have got moxie. They don't sit around fretting about gittin' caught."

"I don't want any part of it."

"Fine you don't git a share of the extra shine we'll make."

"And you can move your still off my land. I've got an education, Mr. Mcleod. I don't necessarily have to consort with the likes of you to make my way in life."

"My, my, the queen has spoken."

"All right stop," shouted Phil.

For a brief moment silence fell over the three of them only to be broken by Mcleod. "You need ta talk some sense to yer woman friend here. We've got this operation all set up so why piddle around with makin' just a few gallons. We need ta make it worth our while."

He didn't know if Mcleod's argument had persuaded him or if it was that bold, irresponsible part of him that he'd last heard from when he decided to abandon everything in Lincoln and pretty much force Martha to join him on this quest for free land, but Phil was leaning towards agreeing with Mcleod that they make the most of their operation. To feel this way surprised him but so did the satisfaction that he felt in him and Catarina having made four gallons of moonshine. It was almost like he had worked the soil, planted a crop and harvested it. Muddled in with this was the realization he could alienate a second woman in his life, but Catarina was different, or so he hoped. He came back. "It'd be just you and me, Mcleod. Like you said, we'd go different places for the supplies."

"And selling the four gallons ah shine? My connections ain't so good here."

Phil sighed. "I may be able to git rid of it in Miles City. I got along good with that fella."

"You could git supplies there too. When you come back with what money is left I'll head over to South Dakota, do my business in a couple different towns." Mcleod paused. "You'll go tomorrow?"

Phil was taken aback. "I was thinkin' we'd run the other two milk cans ah mash 'fore I went."

"Miss Maricelli can do it, can't ya?"

Catarina had mixed feelings about how things had gone but it now seemed to be two against one. She glared briefly at Phil before turning to Mcleod. "I guess I can."

Phil felt as if he had lost control of what had been his idea, not just buying more supplies but the entire operation. It was like Mcleod was directing how things would go and his own greed, and maybe even Catarina's, was making it easy for him. But he needed Mcleod as he flat out didn't know what he was doing until maybe today. And then the naysayer within him called out, trying to convince him that he and Mcleod's impromptu plan was not good. *Yer gonna wind up just like Jack sittin' in jail somewhere and yer gonna lose everything.* The voice was persistent. He tried his best to ignore it.

CHAPTER EIGHTEEN

It was shortly before six the next morning when Phil stopped his truck in front of Catarina's shanty. White smoke was coming from her stovepipe. A gentle morning breeze was laying it over to the west. She appeared in the doorway dressed in brown cotton pants and a gray shirt. She called out, her voice tentative. "Morning."

Phil tossed his head back just catching her eyes before turning back to his truck. "C'mon Ranger dog, you git ta play with Buster today." Ranger jumped down from the cab. He followed Phil towards Catarina. "Ya mind lookin' after Ranger today?"

"Not at all."

Phil stood uneasy for a moment, looking into Catarina's face. He sighed. "I don't suppose there's any point in plowing the same ground as we did last night."

"No, I suppose not. I think I know how things are."

"It matters to me what you say and what you think of me. I'm not like Mcleod."

"I hope not. There's no end to that man's greed. It's going to send him back to prison or worse."

Phil hesitated lest he sound argumentative but the words were already loaded on his tongue. "But you do see how greed can take hold of a person, don't you? For a time, I sensed it in all of us last night."

Seeing where Phil's guilt was taking the conversation, Catarina frowned. "I don't blame you. Starting out, this all seemed like a cavalier lark but now it strikes me as dark and serious. Mcleod is a person that I normally wouldn't associate with, but look at me now."

"I'm sorry Catarina. I never imagined that it would git this way."

Tears had come to her eyes. "The only reason I agreed to this was so I could be closer to you."

A wave of emotion swept over Phil that was mostly good, save for flashes of Martha. "I'd hoped that was the case since you had a job and a way to survive until next year. I'm a scoundrel for dragging you down, Catarina. I really am." He moved to her and encircled her with his arms. She began to cry more freely. She went on, savoring the moment until finally she had sufficiently vented her sadness and fear so as to be able to speak.

"It was brazen of me to say what I did, but it is the truth. I've wanted to tell you for a long time but I thought it too forward, especially with Martha barely gone from here."

"I've had those feelings too but kept them back out of respect for Martha and now – I don't know. Maybe there's a chance she's alive. I wish I knew."

"I hope she is alive. I really do."

For an instant, Phil probed Catarina's eyes for sincerity in what she'd just said but then he caught himself and came back in a voice that likely gave her hope. "Yeah, I do too."

She placed her hands lightly on his chest and stepped back as, once again, the ghost of Martha came between them. "What time do you think you'll be back?"

"By six if things go all right."

"I'll have supper ready."

"People will talk."

"It's your call."

He smiled. "I'll try to be on time." The impulse to kiss her came to him, but it was so laden with shame and guilt for carrying on as they were he could not. Suddenly uneasy, he went on. "Will you be ok running the still?"

She laughed briefly, trying to bleed off her fear. "Chemistry was not my strong suit in school but I'll try to not blow it up."

He contorted his face to show concern.

She came back. "I'll be ok."

He sighed, knowing she was afraid. "Thanksgiving, that'll be the end of it."

"Yes, no more after that."

"I'd better go. The road ta Miles City ain't gittin' any shorter."

"The moonshine is where we left it."

"I'll fetch it."

Phil went around to the far side of Catarina's cabin and retrieved the wooden cask. He set it in the corner of his truck bed up near the cab and began tying it in place with a length of half inch rope.

"It seems pretty bold to be hauling this in plain sight."

Phil laughed and pointed to the side of the barrel. Stenciled in big black letters, it read, Okanogan Valley Apple Cider. "Ain't got nothin' but apple squeezin's, Ma'am."

Catarina shook her head. "Be careful."

Phil jumped down from the bed of his truck and climbed inside. "See ya tonight." At the mouth of the coulee where the road to her house intersected the road to town he looked back. She was still standing in front of her shanty with her arms folded across her chest watching him go. He blew his horn. She waved back big so he'd for sure see that she had. Once again, that emotion came over him, a little stronger than last time.

Phil stopped in Baker and used all of his money but $1.47 filling his tank with gas. It came to him, *I damned sure better be able to sell this shine or I could be walkin' home.* He saw nothing of Wiley Hargis or, for that matter, any law enforcement people; at least those who outwardly made it known that's who they were he didn't. He wrestled the entire way to Miles City with his feelings for Catarina and his frustration in not knowing if he was a widower or not. Mixed in with all of this was his shame for even thinking it in the first place. The only redeeming feature to this mental torture was that the trip seemed to go by quick.

It was exactly 11:30 when Phil parked his truck in front of the Yellowstone Mercantile. Catacorner across the street was the Blue Rock Café. He noted it and said to himself, being positive in the conviction that the proprietor, Silas Orwell, would remember him and buy his shine now that Orosco had blown himself into the hereafter, *I'll make this sale and git somethin' ta eat over there.* The Mercantile was a big white building made of clap boards with a large facade. The store's name had been painted in huge blood red letters across the top of it. Rectangular windows, two on either side of the door, lined the front of the building. Wooden steps, three high, ascended from the dirt street to the door which, for some reason, had never been painted. Phil climbed the steps, opened the shabby looking door and went inside.

The room was cavernous and kind of dark. It had the look of being cool but it wasn't as there were no windows that would open allowing the air to circulate. There were rows and rows of benches and shelves with just about everything a person would need. On the left side of the room it was mostly canned goods, flour, sugar, beans and the like. On the right it was dry goods and tools. Beneath all of this was a hardwood floor that gave slightly causing it to squeak as you walked on it. Phil was squeaking and creaking down the aisle that separated the two sides of the store when a voice hollered out. "Mr. Caldwell, how the hell are ya?"

Phil looked to his right and behind the counter. A middle aged bald man with a black walrus moustache dressed in a dark suit minus the coat was standing there. He felt a sense of relief that the proprietor had not forgotten him. "I'm doin' good, Mr. Orwell."

"That was ah helluva deal ole Pete Orosco blowin' his self up. He made some good product."

Mild shock registered on Phil's face as he remained quiet while quickly looking around before answering.

Orwell laughed. "We're the only ones here."

Phil went on. "Oh, yeah, that was too bad about Mr. Orosco. He was a fine man."

Orwell snickered. "I wasn't talking about his character, just his shine."

Phil tossed his head back but said nothing and laughed politely so as to not embarrass Orwell.

"That man could be a real sonovabitch but I guess I shouldn't speak ill of the dead."

And then it suddenly occurred to Phil that Orwell realized he had crossed over the boundary of common decency and was alone there. It was becoming uncomfortable between them until he validated the store owner's behavior. "Yeah, I believe the man got what was coming to him."

Orwell moved on. "So what brings you all the way over here?"

"I was hopin' ta sell ya some shine and maybe buy ah little corn meal and sugar."

The implication of Phil's words came quickly to Orwell. He grinned, "So yer goin' into business for yer self?"

Phil was reluctant to be known as a moonshiner since his intent was to be done with it by Thanksgiving but the big hail storm had left him no choice, at least in his mind it hadn't. He came back, his voice lacking certainty. "I am, would ya be interested in ah little shine?"

"I'm afraid yer ah little late. The Canadians didn't waste any time after they heard Orosco was dead in finding their way to my door."

Disappointment bordering on devastation smacked Phil's face like a bolt of lightning. "I'll make ya ah good price."

"The Canadians are at $17 and I don't have to worry about it poisoning anybody. No, I don't think I'm interested."

"I'll let ya have my product for $15. It's good stuff."

Orwell shook his head. "I don't know. I've got a good thing goin' with these boys and to be honest with ya they're the kinda people you don't wanna git crosswise with."

"Alright $14, that's as low as I can go."

Orwell sighed heavily. "I hate to see a man grovel. It's kinda like ah starvin' dog, I can't turn 'em away. So, I'll give ya ah try, for $14 but I gotta taste it first and if I don't like it, the deal's off. And I only want a few gallons."

The lie slid off Phil's tongue as slick as ice cream. "That's all I got left. Sold the rest."

Orwell looked as if he resented being pressured, nonetheless he went on, "Pull yer truck around back. I'll meet ya there."

"All right."

Phil drove his truck down the alley between the Mercantile and a doctor's office next door. He went through an open gate into a storage yard surrounded by a board fence that was eight feet high. To his right were piles of posts and barbed wire stacked against the fence. On the south and west sides of the compound were open face half sheds that protected from the elements piles of various sized boards and sacks of cement and things such as block salt and feed for livestock. Orwell, however, was motioning towards a small wooden storage shed near the back door of the main building. As Phil turned his truck in that direction Orwell went inside the shed. Moments later he reappeared with an empty quart Mason jar. Phil turned his truck off next to the crusty store owner. "Alright, let's see whatcha got?"

Phil got out, took the jar and hopped up onto the bed of the truck. He poured a healthy sample of the shine and handed it down to Orwell who first smelled of it. His expression was unchanged. He then poured a few drops onto his fingers and rubbed it between them. Finally, he took a sip and swallowed it. And then it was as if he was reviewing the messages that his senses had sent back to his brain, his face blank as a freshly cleaned blackboard. Phil could take it no more. "So how's she settin'?"

"For $14, right?"

"Yes sir."

"Bring yer barrel inside the shed."

Phil wrestled the 20 gallon barrel with its paltry four gallons sloshing around inside it from the back of the truck and took it into the shed. A wooden counter extended from the left wall while shelves filled with quart Mason jars of moonshine lined the right and back walls. Orwell cleared a space on the counter as Phil approached. "Set 'er down here."

Phil set the cask on its side with the spigot in position to pour. Orwell held the jar he'd just drunk from under it and filled it up. He set it on the counter and began screwing the lid on. "Well, there's one."

Phil pulled another empty jar from a cardboard box on the counter and set it within reach of Orwell. "There should be 16."

"We'll see."

The barrel had not leaked any on the long rough ride. It yielded the 16 quarts that Phil hoped would be in it but the $80 he'd also hoped for was fantasy. But that was not the only disappointment. "Twenty-five pounds that's the best ya can do on the sugar?"

Orwell grimaced. "It is. Hoover's boys are stickin' their noses into everybody's business these days. You'd think as tough as times are the sonsabitches wouldn't begrudge ah man ah drink ta ease the stress ah goin' broke."

Phil resigned himself to how things were. He parroted Orwell. "Yeah, you'd think so."

"Alright then, ya got $45 coming and ya got yer sugar and ah hunderd pounds ah corn meal." Orwell reached into his pocket and pulled out a wad of bills.

Phil noted the money and just beyond it all of the quart jars of moonshine on the shelves. The words escaped him. "Whaddya git for ah quart?"

Orwell scowled at him. "Six bucks and ah lotta worry the Feds are gonna swoop in here and shut my store down and throw me in jail and leave my wife and kids ta fend for themselves."

Phil's discussion with Catarina about greed came to mind. "Well, why do it? Don't ya make a good enough living with the Mercantile?"

Orwell acted as if he hadn't heard Phil. He counted out the $45 and gave it to him. "If you got anymore shine yer willin' ta let go for $14 I'll take it off yer hands."

Phil thought, *I bet you would*, but he nodded so as to leave that door open, and said simply, "Alright. Appreciate the business."

Orwell nodded. "I better git back inside."

As they stepped from the shed the back door to the Mercantile opened. Two men came out and started towards them. Orwell immediately became nervous. "You better go."

"Those the Canadians?"

"You better skedaddle while you can."

Phil climbed in his truck and fired it up. He had to make a loop in the ware yard in order to get turned around and headed for the exit, as he did he glanced over at the Canadians who were staring intently at him. He made eye contact with them but it right away gave him a bad feeling so he looked toward the exit and accelerated the truck. As he came onto the street there was a brief moment when common sense was winning out against his hunger. *Those boys appear ta be ruffians. I'd be smart ta just head fer home and eat some ah Catarina's cookin' tonight.* But then the ornery side of him entered into it. *To hell with them fellas. A man's got a right ta do business and besides that I'm hungry.* Phil parked his truck in front of the Blue Rock Café and went inside. The room was like a tunnel with a lunch counter on the left side and tables and chairs on the right. There was however, a table next to a window facing the street with a clear view of the Mercantile's front door. He sat down and looked out. *Well, I guess I'll know purty soon if they got an interest in me.*

"Special today is roast beef."

Phil jerked his head around in response to the monotone voice. An older red haired woman was standing next to his table. She had watery, bloodshot green eyes and wrinkles in her face so deep, yet perfectly contoured, they reminded him of a field that had been corrugated so as to accommodate flood irrigation. He came back, trying to not look at either her eyes or wrinkles, "Whaddaya git with that?"

The woman sighed as if he had asked a stupid question. "It comes with mashed spuds, green beans, biscuits and dessert."

"Any kind ah dessert?"

She frowned. "No, it's peach cobbler today."

Phil thought to ask if that included a scoop of ice cream, but seeing how she was he did not. "I'll have the special and a glass ah water."

At last she was able to write his order down on her palm sized ticket book. And then she simply walked away, saying nothing, not even making eye contact lest she allow him to linger in their torment. A clock encased in dark oak wood hung on the wall behind the counter. It had bold, black Roman numerals with equally prominent hands behind a glass cover above a brass pendulum that metered out the time, 12:17. Phil noted most of the seats were empty. *Maybe the locals know somethin' I don't.* He watched as the old lady looked through the portal to the kitchen and laid his ticket on the shelf. "Special." There was no response. She leaned further into the cook's domain. "Hey Louie, special." The cook came back with something indiscernible, at least to Phil it was. He turned his attention to the Mercantile. The strange truck, the one that had come after he'd driven around back was still there. Common sense somehow bobbed to the surface in the muddy waters of his mind. *Shit, I probably shudda just got on down the road.* He sighed, still looking out the window. *Well, I'll eat, however good this grub will be and then I'll gas up and git the hell outta here.*

The old lady returned, silent like a ghost, with a glass of water, silverware and a napkin. Phil pulled his hands back while keeping his eyes focused on the table as if she needed his visual assistance in setting the items down. He glanced at her. "Thank you." And then she went away as before saying nothing.

The clock on the wall read 12:25. He'd been maintaining a vigil on the Mercantile such that he was unaware of the old lady's presence until she set his food in front of him. She'd taken a half step to leave before he could ask, "Can I git some meat sauce?"

His request brought her to a complete halt whereupon she looked over at him. "Have you even tried the roast yet?"

"No, but I put sauce on all my meat."

"You should try it. Louie spices everything. It ain't yer normal roast."

Phil sighed, but did as the old lady had asked and cut a bite of the meat. He chewed several times and swallowed. It had a peculiar sweet taste. He looked up at her. "I guess we'll give 'er ah go just like it is."

Abruptly, she looked out the window squinting her eyes against the light. "That who yer lookin' for?"

Phil registered genuine surprise as he'd been looking directly at the old lady and had not seen the Canadians emerge from the Mercantile. He came back spontaneously. "What?"

She nodded out the window. "Those two, they're not good people."

Phil followed the old lady's painful eyes. "I don't know those men."

"Oh, I thought maybe the way you've had yer face glued to the window since ya came in here you might ah been lookin' for 'em."

Phil said nothing as he watched the Canadians who were standing beside their truck looking and pointing across the street to his truck.

For whatever reason, maybe she sensed his fear, the old lady had not yet left. "It appears they got an interest in yer truck."

Phil played dumb. "Or yer café."

The old lady scoffed. "That ain't likely."

"You know those fellas?"

"They eat here once in a while. The big one with the beard is Frank something and the other shorter guy goes by his last name, Connors. They're bootleggers."

"How do you know that?"

"You'd be surprised what people talk about when I'm around. I guess they don't think I can hear."

Phil managed a weak grin. "Well, I guess they'd be wrong."

The old lady lowered her voice slightly and leaned towards the table allowing Phil to scrutinize the veins on the surface of her eyes. "Listen, about a month ago a fella named Hightower got killed in a car wreck out east ah here. There was rumors he got run off the road. Not long after it happened I heard these two whisperin' about it."

Common sense yelled at Phil again. *You dumbass, ya shudda left 'fore they got ya pinned down in here, all because you had ta feed yer face.* And then he came back in a sober, worried voice that kind of trailed off, "I appreciate yer enlightenin' me."

The front door opened causing the old lady to walk away.

Phil looked out the window. The Canadians were sitting in their truck. Fear pulsed through him. *Shit, what she says is true. They're just waitin' for me ta leave.* He turned back to his food and began to eat, it had become tasteless. *Maybe I should just go talk to 'em.* But then the naysayer in him bowed up. *You can't let 'em chase ya outta here, if ya do you'll be doin' things Mcleod's way, drivin' two days ta Denver where the cops'll be lookin' for him and anybody else with him.*

There was a Remington Arms calendar to the right and below the clock on the wall. The top half of it was a picture of a man in a skiff on a lake hunting ducks at dawn. Phil pretended to be looking at the picture as the old lady approached. It was 12:46. She looked at his plate. The food was about half gone but he'd not eaten anything in the last five minutes.

"Ya want yer dessert?"

"No, just my check."

She reached in her apron pocket for the bill and laid it on the table. It was a fluid motion her head swiveling, never stopping, in the direction she intended to go while saying, "Good luck to ya, Mister." And then she was gone.

Phil left fifty cents for the special and a dime tip before going outside. The Canadians were still sitting in their truck. Cigarette smoke was drifting out of the driver's side window. *The hell with 'em*, thought Phil. He opened the door of his truck and got in. He backed out and drove by their truck. They pretended to not be interested but he'd gone only a short ways when he saw in his mirror they were following him. At the edge of town he stopped for gas at a little store that was mostly there by itself leaving the Canadians with no inconspicuous place to stop other than to pull into the store and buy something. But they did not stop. They kept on going at a good clip like they were glad to be leaving Miles City and eager to get on to their next destination. Even though Phil watched them pass by they acted as if they had no interest in him. It wasn't until their truck had become a black dot on the horizon and sank from sight that Phil allowed himself to relax. *Maybe the old lady is wrong about those boys.*

After putting exactly five gallons of gas in his truck, Phil went inside and gave the clerk $1.65 for the gas and a nickel for a bottle of coco-cola. And then he set off in the same direction the Canadians had gone as that was the road home. He finished the coco-cola and a Lucky Strike well before he crossed over the Powder River which was about a third of the way to Baker. He told himself, because he needed to believe it, when he was a couple miles past the Powder, *I'll bet I'm such small potatoes compared to those boys they've just gone on down the road.* He drove on, feeling mostly at ease pondering how Catarina had faired with running the still by herself. And then it was just after the road had started to hug Locate Creek pretty tight and there were places that people had pulled off to camp that Phil's left eye nearly jumped out of its socket. "Those sorry sonsabitches." He did not slow down, but it was no matter, as the Canadians were after him and quickly closing the distance. On gravel roads such as this one, he seldom drove over 25 miles per hour, but he had incentive now to see just how fast his truck would go. He pulled the throttle lever down, not as far as it would go but close to it. The little Model T truck responded gradually getting up to 37 miles per hour. He was putting up a decent dust cloud and pulling away slightly from the Canadians when he heard a loud pop behind him and, at the same instant, the seat's upholstery a few inches to the right of his upper torso ruptured as did the windshield. "Shit, these bastards aim ta kill me." Phil jerked the throttle lever as far down as it would go. The speedometer climbed to 42 miles per hour and stalled there, but he was beginning to pull away. His heart was pounding furiously like it needed to keep pace with the pistons of his truck's engine. Driving this fast was a new experience and he was not doing particularly well at keeping the truck stable in the thick gravel. At times, its wheels would break loose and the truck would begin to fish tail causing Phil to frantically counter steer. But he had no choice; he kept on as he was until suddenly another loud pop sounded behind him that was instantly accompanied by a stinging jolt under his right arm which uncontrollably fell away from the steering wheel. Phil grimaced in pain as he struggled to maintain control of the truck. He had nothing to fight back with except his truck and it was incapable of out running them. And then the old lady's words echoed in his mind, *he got run off the road.* It would be a gamble but what choice did he have? Up to this point the road had followed in a general way the sinuosity of the creek, but now it suddenly straightened. In his mind Phil could see it play out, if only they would fall for it. He had maybe a half mile to lure them in. Through the pain, he willed his right hand to push the throttle lever up. He then slumped over the wheel as if he were dead or dying. At first the Canadians stayed back, but then they gained so quickly on his truck which appeared to be in danger of running off the side of the road away from the creek, that they surged ahead pulling alongside of him. With his forehead resting on the top of the steering wheel, Phil could see from the corner of his eye the instant they were even with him. He'd prepositioned his hands, his left in an underhanded grip at about nine o'clock on the steering wheel and his right, hidden by his slumped over torso, on the throttle. And then, just as Frank the bearded guy started to extend his pistol out the window, Phil took his shot. With one adrenaline fueled burst he pulled the throttle down while jerking the steering wheel and ramming his truck into the Canadians. The impact caught them by surprise. Their truck careened violently toward the creek side edge of the road. Connors tried to counter steer but Phil's momentum would not allow it. Frank got off one more shot from his .38 caliber Colt that went over Phil's head and out the corner of his truck's cab. But it was a parting shot, so to speak, as their truck went off the road and down a steep embankment rolling over and coming to rest on its top in the creek. Phil's rage in pushing them over nearly caused him to follow as his left front wheel dipped perilously close to the edge, but he recovered and went on down the road not looking back. In a couple of miles, when some of the adrenaline had filtered from his system, he became aware of the wetness on his right side and looked down at his blood soaked shirt. A different kind of fear now came over him. *How am I gonna explain this? And the damage to my truck?* But then this fear was suddenly overshadowed by the realization that he might have just killed two men. He felt himself becoming sick but was able to drive another mile or so before having to abruptly pull off the road beside the creek. There he bailed out of his truck, dropped to his knees and spewed the Blue Rock special over the yellow grass before him. He remained on his hands and knees until he was sure he was through and then he went to the creek and removed his shirt. The bullet had plowed a furrow across the muscle mass beneath his arm. In a way it reminded him of the old lady's wrinkles. He soaked his shirt in the cold creek water and washed off as much of the blood as he could. The wound had started to clot but still oozed some blood. He took off one of his boots and his sock. After rinsing the sock several times in the creek and squeezing the water out of it he pressed it along the length of his wound and tied it in place with some twine that had been lying on the floor of his truck's cab. He then washed as much of the blood as he could out of his shirt and put it back on. He felt a little better, but he still had a long way to go.

It was fortunate that he was relatively new to the area and he lived so far out as, up to this point, he had met no one on the road that he recognized. However, he knew it would be foolish to drive through town as Wiley Hargis might see him and would no doubt be curious about the bullet holes and damage to his truck. He therefore skirted around Baker picking up the road home a couple miles north of town. Blood still seeped from his wound. Much of it was captured by the sock and when the road was smooth it would begin to congeal, but it was a poor county and road maintenance wasn't what it should have been. It was nearly six o'clock and he still had about ten miles to go. He felt sickish and weak and his right side was consumed by a burning pain. As much as possible, he tried to use only his left arm in driving the truck. On he went, getting closer to Catarina's and the pampering he suspected she would give him. Then, just as he topped a rise in the road the inevitable happened. "Ah dammit, not now, not this close." Up ahead parked at the edge of the road and next to his field was not only Karl Walters but Edith too. Karl recognized Phil's truck and stood waiting in the road for him to stop and visit. *He's gonna think it peculiar as hell if I keep on going but what do I tell him.* The smile on Karl's face suddenly went away. *Aw shit, he already sees the damage.* Phil's mind exploded in panic as he brought his truck to a halt next to Karl.

"What the hell happened to yer truck? You hit ah deer?"

It was reflex mostly that Phil instantly thought to agree with Karl that it was a collision with a deer that had mangled his left front fender and knocked his left headlight completely off. But then came the part where he would have to explain how the deer had shot a hole in his windshield. Fortunately for him, common sense and a need to be free of the worry of someone finding out took charge of his tongue. "No Karl, some fellas shot me and tried to run me off the road, but I got the better of 'em."

Karl's face registered shock whereas Edith's was more like she'd just been allowed access to a buffet of juicy gossip that would help deter the loneliness of her existence. Those long hot days where the heat distorted images at a distance and the only sound was the grasshoppers crackling flight. Those days where tiny springs of sweat sprang up on your forehead and temple and discharged their saltiness down into your eyes and across your cheeks. Those days where as a woman you wished you could shed that long skirt and dress like a man. On those boring days, she could tell of Phil's misfortune. And then Karl came back, "Are ya alright?"

"Not entirely."

"How so?"

"They clipped me in my side."

"Did ya go to the doctor?"

"No, doctors cost money. I doctored it myself."

"So where'd all this happen?"

"Just east ah the Powder."

Karl shook his head. "Hell's bells you've come quite a ways bleedin' like ya are. Did ya know these fellas?"

So as to be able to hide his lie, Phil manufactured a grimace as if the pain from his wound had suddenly increased. "No, hell no. I'd never seen these two yahoos until they pulled outta the bushes along Locate Creek and started after me. I think they was probably road agents lookin' ta rob me. There's gotten to be more ah that kind a thing ya know since times has gotten so tough."

"Oh, don't ya know it." Karl paused and came right back. "Did ya report this ta Wiley?"

"No, I just wanna go home."

Karl looked incredulous like he'd just been lied to, but then it was Edith's turn to offer up a smoke screen for her words. "Maybe you should stop by Miss Maricelli's since she lives so close to you and let her know of your injury. Maybe she could check in on you, just to make sure you're ok."

It was apparent to Phil that Edith was looking to expand the buffet. *She could give ah tinker's dam about my well-being but she's dying to know what's between me and Catarina.* Unknowingly, however, she had given him justification to go to Catarina's this evening. "I believe I may do that. Miss Maricelli has become a good neighbor now that Martha has passed on."

A poker player, Edith was not. At the mention of Martha being dead her eyes lit up like she had just drawn out to a full house. "So what do you propose to do?"

"Do? Whaddaya mean?"

"About Martha, I mean are you gonna stay married to her?"

Karl snapped. "Edith, for hell sake's. The man's just been shot."

"I'm sorry, Phil. I didn't mean to pry. It's just that Martha was my friend and I, well I don't know what I was thinking."

Like hell you didn't know. He said aloud, his words purposeful. "I suppose there'll come a time when I'll have ta legally dissolve what we had."

"Divorce? You mean you'd divorce her?"

"Dammit Edith. Leave the man alone. Don't answer that, Phil. We're goin home. Hope ya heal up alright."

"Thanks Karl."

"Git in the truck, Edith. We're leavin'."

Phil put his truck in gear and headed on down the road.

CHAPTER NINETEEN

Had Edith Walters kept tabs on Catarina's shanty that night her gossip buffet would have overflowed. It was a night that like good sour mash had been a long time in the making. Catarina had insisted that she clean and dress Phil's wound properly and too, she would not allow him to go home. And so they'd lain on her bed, fully clothed throughout the night. Sometime in the early morning she consciously rested her hand on his chest. For a good while after that, he lay there awake listening to her breath and savoring the weight of her hand over his heart. But Martha's ghost had been joined by those of the Canadians and together they ruined any fantasies he might have entertained. Finally, when it was barely light Catarina's rooster announced the new day. Phil gently edged from beneath her hand so as to not disturb her and went outside to the privy. He was nearly back to the shanty when the door opened.

She smiled. "Did Clyde wake you?"

For an instant, the old Phil thought to be flippant and joke about Clyde needing to be Sunday dinner but the image of the Canadians going over the edge into the creek and most likely being dead would not leave his mind. He shook his head. "No, truth be told I been waitin' on him."

"I'm sorry. Just too much pain?"

"Yeah, I guess you could say that. I got more on my mind than what'll fit there."

"You want to talk about it?"

"I don't know that talkin' will git rid of it."

"Probably not, but you might be able to store some of your troubles on a shelf you don't often go to."

Phil laughed briefly in a somber, serious way. "Those fellas are likely dead because of me. Something like that might require a whole new root cellar with a steel door."

Catarina shook her head as if she was mystified. "They were trying to kill you."

"I know. It's just this whole mess. If I wasn't trying to bail myself out makin' shine I never would have gone to Miles City and those fellas and me wudda never met."

"But what else could you do? Give it all back to the bank and just walk away?"

"At least I wudda been within the law. And I wouldn't ah had any black marks against me come judgement day."

"I didn't know you were religious."

"I'm not a bible thumper, but I don't know that I want to bet against all those that are."

A gentle cool breeze out of the east came up. Catarina folded her arms across her chest. She sighed. "You're a good man. God would have to be pretty narrow minded to send you to hell."

Phil laughed. "Well then, I hope you've got some sway with him."

She stepped close and took hold of his arm on his uninjured side. "What you need is some of my sourdough hotcakes and hot coffee."

In his mind he did not feel much better but it was clear that he'd exhausted her reassurances, at least for now he had. He came back, "Maybe so," and allowed her to lead him away from his pity party there in the gray of dawn.

He was sore and kind of weak and didn't much feel like working the still but he didn't feel good either about having her work it by herself so he stayed on, his truck parked right there in front of her shanty for Edith Walters to see, and as it turned out, Wiley Hargis.

They were in the process of mixing up another twenty gallons of mash with the supplies Phil had bought in Miles City when Catarina suddenly gasped, "Oh my God, that looks like the Sheriff's car."

Phil looked in the direction of the rooster tail following the big black car down on the main road. He sighed heavily. "We better git down to yer house. He gits close ta here and he'll smell the still."

It was a race, so to speak, that Wiley won as he arrived first at her place. He'd just knocked a second time and was standing there looking at Phil's truck when they all of a sudden came around the corner of the house.

Phil looked Wiley in the eye. "I suppose you've talked to Karl Walters."

"Yeah, him and Edith was in town this morning and I happened to run into them. Your name came up and I guess you know the tale they told me."

"Those boys was out ta rob me."

"They'd be purty damned greedy if they was."

A sudden cold, sweaty feeling came over Phil. "Whaddaya mean?"

"I called the Sheriff over in Miles City. They fished those boys outta the crik last night just before dark. They had eleven hundred and fifty-two dollars cash money on'em and ten gallons a Canadian whiskey. So I don't know that they was lookin' ta rob you. The Sheriff over there was wonderin' if it was the other way around."

Phil exploded with anger. "The man's a damned fool. I got a bullet hole in my side. I'm tellin' ya Sheriff, those boys came after me. I had no choice but to run 'em off the road. Just look at the bullet holes in my truck."

"Yeah, I saw those and I'm inclined to believe they attacked you, but my nose is wrinklin' up. There's somethin' that smells foul about this whole affair. Those boys had ta have some reason for chasin' after ya like that."

"Well, beats the hell outta me what it was."

"You know ah suspicious person might think you were some kind of a threat to those fella's livelihood. And I gotta tell ya, it's a long ways out here so I had plenty ah time ta cogitate on that possibility and to be honest with ya Mr. Caldwell, it makes some sense to me."

"Maybe they got me confused with somebody else because I'm no threat to bootleggers."

"I never said they was bootleggers."

The blood drained from Phil's face. "You said they had ten gallons of Canadian whiskey. Why else would they have that much whiskey if they weren't going to sell it?"

Wiley nodded and reached into his shirt pocket for his pack of cigarettes, shook one out and lit it. He took several long drags, clouding the air in front of him with smoke. "You say they shot ya?"

Catarina jumped in. "They did Sheriff. I can testify to that." And then her sudden bold demeanor wilted as her face turned red.

Wiley came back, his voice respectful but flavored with a hint of smugness. "I believe you, Miss Maricelli." And then out of the blue he went on, casting his bait out into the pond. "I heard you might be comin' ta town to teach this year."

Catarina was caught off guard. "You did?"

"I know ah lotta people."

"Actually Sheriff, I've decided against that. I don't want to leave my place unattended."

"Oh, well that makes sense especially if ah person can afford ta do that."

"Yes, I've got a little money put aside."

Phil had been studying Wiley's face as he talked to Catarina. *He knows. Sure as shit he knows. He's just toying with us.*

And then, like he was making his way across a frozen river that was breaking up by hopping from one solid piece of ice to another, Wiley came back at Phil, "I reckon for now I can tell the sheriff over in Miles City that those boys in the crik got what was comin' to'em. But you should know that fella has a real suspicious mind."

Phil sighed. "Well Sheriff, I'm tellin' ya the truth."

Wiley took a drag from his cigarette. He was smiling. It was the kind a person flashed when they didn't want to call you a liar to your face. He came back. "I guess you never said what the nature of yer business in Miles City was."

"I'd heard that ah man might be able to git seed for plantin' winter wheat on credit over there. Turned out not to be true."

Wiley kept on smiling like it had been carved in stone. "It's too damned bad old Pete Orosco's still blew up otherwise ya might ah got more work haulin' coal."

Phil's heart rate jumped a little more. *He's gittin' some pleasure outta teasin' me like he is. He don't no more believe that story about there bein' nothin' but coal in them sacks than he does pigs can fly.* Phil played along. "Aw it's no matter. That didn't pay fer beans."

Wiley put his cigarette back into his mouth and cupped his right hand over the butt of his pistol like he needed to reassure himself it was still there. He then rotated his head around, peering out from beneath the brim of his peaked Stetson hat as if he was looking for something. Silence, save for the grasshoppers and horse flies, descended upon them like an English fog. And then to justify himself, he came back with a statement of the obvious. "She's ah hot one today, ain't she?"

Phil thought to say nothing and leave Wiley's words hanging there but the badge on Wiley's shirt intimidated him. "It sure is. We need rain bad."

Wiley pressed his lips down on his cigarette and drew in the smoke until his lungs were full and then, as if he'd lost the use of his hands, he blew the smoke out one side of his mouth while leaving the cigarette in the other. His eyes had come to rest on Phil's truck. He appeared to be examining it like a doctor would his patient just prior to rendering his diagnosis. There was no doubt, at least in Phil's mind there wasn't, that Wiley was getting some satisfaction in making him squirm. Finally, he removed the cigarette from his mouth and faced Phil. He sighed. "I guess for now we'll leave things as they are, but just don't lose sight of the fact that the sheriff in Miles City may want to talk to ya."

Phil frowned slightly and shrugged his shoulders. "I reckon if he wants ta burn the county's gas driving all the way over here, I'll tell him just like I told you."

"He's ah suspicious man. There's lots ah moonshinin' goin on over there. I told him you were smarter than ta git involved in such activity but he didn't believe me."

"He's got no call to think badly of me."

"Maybe not but he does."

Wylie had started toward his car when Phil decided to retaliate and make him feel uneasy. "I don't suppose you've found out anything new about Martha, have ya?"

He stopped and looked back at Phil. "I wudda told ya if I had."

Phil thought to get angry and yell back. *There's some real crime for ya. Why don't ya git off yer sorry ass and figure out who took my wife?* But he did not. They watched as Wylie drove off. It wasn't until he'd reached the main road and gone a ways that Catarina said what they were both thinking. "He doesn't believe you. I suspect he's going to be watching you."

"Probably so."

"What are you going to do?"

Phil shook his head and sighed. "I don't know."

CHAPTER TWENTY

It was the fifteenth of September and they were finished processing all of the mash that they'd had funds to make. The end result of all their subterfuge and trepidation was about 70 gallons of shine worth $1,400.00 if they could transport it to Denver without getting caught. Phil didn't dare go back to Miles City which was much closer, nor did he want to try Bismarck where Jack still languished in jail. They had the means to make a lot of money, if only they had the courage or a temporary lapse in common sense. But therein lay the problem. There were lots of people getting busted for moonshine. Phil was certain that not only the sheriff in Miles City but Wiley Hargis as well suspected him. Even Mcleod stayed away from both Catarina and Phil's place. Phil had followed Orosco's practice of using the mail to communicate with him. Mcleod was insistent that Phil make a run to Denver and take all of their moonshine. He'd talked by phone to a man who owned a big hotel and restaurant with a 'speakeasy' in the basement. The man said he'd buy all they could bring.

Phil looked across the table to Catarina. "I can't believe we've painted ourselves into a corner like we have."

"I know. We've got to end this soon, one way or another. I'm fearful there will come a time when the Sheriff or the Feds are going to show up here and want to search my property. To tell you the truth, I'm so tired of the worry I'd just as soon dump our shine, tear the still apart and just be done with it."

"That would mean I'd be throwing away my only chance to save my farm equipment and my place. Hell, I don't even have enough money to eat on."

"They still need a teacher in town. You could live here and take care of my place." She hesitated briefly and then added, "We could be together on weekends."

Phil paused and looked into her eyes to acknowledge the last part of what she'd said before shaking his head. "I appreciate the offer but I'd still default on my loan at the bank, not to mention all the gossip it would create."

"So you're going?"

"I've invested what little money I had in this, everything, hell even my soul. I've killed men because of this. I can't give up on it now."

"If they catch you they'll take it all away and then some. You'll have nothing."

"And if I don't go, I'll have nothing." He paused and smiled directly at her. "Don't forget, it'll fill yer pantry too."

"It's not worth it."

"We're beatin' ah dead horse. I'm gonna load the truck today and leave early tomorrow."

Catarina sighed. "If I'm going to share in the profits I should go with you."

"Somebody's got to tend yer chickens and take care ah Buster and Ranger."

Catarina rested her elbows on the table. She closed her eyes and looked down while gently massaging her forehead with the tips of her fingers as if she was in painful thought.

With her eyes still closed she began to purge her mind. "I was lured here by the promise of free land, so to speak. Deep down, I'd hoped that I'd find my soul mate too. And now, all because of a damned hail storm and the law, I might be deprived of both. It just doesn't seem fair." Tears began to seep from her closed eyes.

Phil reached across the table and took hold of her hands. "I won't let 'em catch me."

Catarina opened her eyes and smiled weakly. "You'd better not."

The sun was not quite above the horizon when Phil parked his truck in front of her shanty all loaded and ready to go. He'd spent the night at his place, as he usually did, even though purveyors of gossip like Edith Walters had made it fact that he routinely did otherwise as Catarina was a loose woman, a hussy chasing after a grieving widower who shamelessly was allowing his self to be caught. "Let's go Ranger dog." Phil was not quite to her door when it opened. He said in a jovial tone seemingly ignoring the gravity of what he was doing. "I see Clyde has routed you outta bed this mornin'."

Catarina played along. "He did. He's not one to shirk his duties."

"I brought Ranger."

"I'm sure Buster will be pleased."

And then he cut to it. "I'm shootin' ta be back in five days."

"That seems like such a long time."

"It is, but unless they shrink the road between here and Denver, I don't see it being anything less."

It was a mutual thing, that expectation they should kiss one another because of their situation. Had there been the degree of familiarity between them that the gossipers knew to be true it would have been easy for either one of them to initiate. But that was not the case. They stood awkwardly looking at one another until finally Phil stepped closer and wrapped his arms around her, his hands immersed in her long black hair hanging down. She received his kiss in a hungry way like it was the sustenance of life itself.

She drew back slightly. "Please be careful."

And then he said, his words clearly coated with a false courage; "You can rest assured I have no intention of ending up in some law dog's caboose."

CHAPTER TWENTY-ONE

It was early afternoon on the second day of his journey that Phil finally arrived in Denver. He'd not tried to take any back roads or engage in any kind of deception other than the tank beneath the bed of his truck. In his mind, it was the man who conducted himself in a guilty manner that drew attention and got caught. He had, however, taken funds from the sale of the shine in Miles City sufficient to repair his headlight so he would be legal and could drive at night. His crumpled fender and windshield, which had morphed into a massive spider web on the driver's side, he simply removed. Nonetheless, Mcleod had become incensed. *You damned fool. Do you know how much mash we cudda made with that money?* They'd nearly come to blows over it.

There was little semblance between Denver and where he had come from. It was a mecca for commerce and a fulcrum between the plains to the east and the massive timber covered mountains to the west. Business people and weary travelers converged daily on the busy city and many of these individuals wanted a good meal, a bed and a drink when they got there. The Front Range Hotel provided all three.

Phil did as Mcleod had instructed and parked about a block away from the hotel. The street was alive with automobiles. In his opinion too many of them were honking their horns unnecessarily. People were like ants on the sidewalks, coming and going to do whatever ants did. He felt out of place amongst the smartly dressed men in their suits and derby hats and the women in their fancy dresses, some of which would have been considered risqué in Baker. It occurred to him as he walked towards the hotel that he wasn't the same person that had lived in Lincoln. He hadn't been gone two full days and already he missed the solitude of his homestead, the call of the meadow larks and the peacefulness of watching the sun rise and set. But most of all, he missed Catarina. And then before the emotion of her image had passed, his mind suddenly exploded. Not twenty feet away coming out of the door of the Front Range Hotel was Martha on the arm of a man. She had not seen him yet. However, the man who was not particularly handsome but wore expensive looking clothes had noticed Phil staring at them. He stopped and whispered to Martha. She looked over and instantly her face became ashen, a chameleon of shame, fear, regret and finally anger.

She said, not caring who heard, "So you've found me."

The indifference in her words struck home. It was not what he'd expected her to say, but then for the longest time he'd believed she was dead. And now it was as if she'd gone between his ribs with a stiletto and pierced his heart. He felt sick and bewildered. He looked at her and then at the man, almost frail with wire rim glasses and a thin salt and pepper moustache. But the man's physical appearance did not match the defiance in his eyes. It was the man's look that enabled Phil to push out some of the hurt. "I take it you haven't missed me."

Martha held to her demeanor of indifference. "No, I haven't. It was over between us a long time ago, Phil."

"If that's how you felt, why not just tell me? Why leave in such a cruel way? I could've died in that well."

"But you didn't."

"You didn't know that I wouldn't."

"I knew Jack Schneider was coming over later that day."

"But he didn't come."

A smirk came to the frail man's face. Phil lashed out. "This asshole needs ta go on about his business while he's still able."

The frail man laughed. "Sir, you will be sorry that you referred to me in that manner." He paused and shook his head emphatically. "Yes, you will regret those words."

Phil took a step towards the man. "Well, maybe you can just start dishin' out that regret right now."

Martha blocked Phil's path with her arm. "No Phil, please." And then she turned to her friend. "Marshal, there's no need for a scene. I'll meet you at your office in just a little while."

The frail man scoffed. "Don't be long."

"I won't."

When the man was beyond hearing, Phil came back; "I guess I just don't understand this Martha."

"I knew you wouldn't. Even in Lincoln you were happy with our simple little lives mundane as they were. But then when you became obsessed with this notion of homesteading, that was too much. I hate that place and all the loneliness and poverty it brought. I hate not having money or being able to talk to people. You don't seem to mind that."

"It's temporary Martha. Someday things will be different."

Martha laughed in a derisive way. "How long do you think we're going to live? I want to enjoy today Phil, not endure it on the hope that someday things will be better."

The determination to be free of him was clearly in her face and voice. There was not a hint of remorse in either. It caused the pain within him to surge and his mind's eye to go back to that day at the corral. "Why the chicken blood? Why make me think you were dead? It's like you wanted to deprive me of any hope that I'd ever get you back. But now, it's like you just wanted to hurt me."

For a moment there was compassion, maybe even regret in her eyes but she stopped short of apologizing. "I didn't want you to look for me. I just wanted you to think I was dead and gone."

"That was cruel. Why not just ask me for a divorce?"

Martha snorted and tossed her head. "You wouldn't have agreed to it." She paused briefly and then went on in a haughty tone, "You know Phil, as for you being the grieving widower I have information to the contrary."

"What are you talking about?"

"Catarina Maricelli, that's what I'm talking about."

"You've been talking to Edith Walters."

"She's my friend. She enabled me to correspond with the outside world until Marshal came to my rescue."

Phil scoffed. "I knew she had a hand in all of this and Pete Orosco too."

Martha appeared to gloat. "Marshal knows lots of people. You'd be wise not to anger him."

"So you did go out through Orosco's place."

"Yes, we even stopped for lunch. His wife was very gracious."

Phil thought to come back with something derogatory about Orosco but caught himself. There was no point prolonging the animosity. It was over between them. The woman standing before him was not who he had married and truth be told, maybe he was a different man. He cut to it. "So you want a divorce?"

"You know I do."

"Well, I suppose yer friend has got more means than I do so if you wanna git the papers drawn up and mail 'em to me, I'll sign 'em." And then just to be flippant like none of this hurt, he threw in; "Why, you'll be ah free woman in no time."

"I'll get the paperwork started today." She paused before adding, her voice faltering just slightly; "I won't be coming for any of my things. Marshal provides for me quite well."

"All right."

"Goodbye Phil." And with that she walked away in the same direction as the frail man had gone.

Phil started to say goodbye but couldn't, even after all that had happened, allow himself to bring such finality to their relationship. He watched her until she disappeared around the corner of the next building before going inside the hotel and taking a seat in the lobby to collect his self. He sat there a good while stunned by her bitterness, such that he questioned himself as a man in all ways imaginable. Gradually, his confidence in what he had with Catarina began to edge out the feelings of inadequacy and sorrow that engulfed his mind to the point he said to himself; *Hell, maybe Martha did me ah favor.*

In addition to the Front Range providing their guests with moonshine and beer they provided limousine service to and from the train station. It was a fancy car, a burgundy colored 1929 Cadillac with whitewall tires. When not in use it was stored in a large garage behind the hotel. It was here that Phil was told to bring his truck with the product. The unloading of his shine went fairly quick. A rubber hose was attached to the valve in the bottom of the tank beneath his truck's bed and fed into ten gallon wooden casks, one after another until all 70 gallons had been drained. A man named Harvey, just Harvey, did everything. When the barrels were all locked away in a storage room off of the garage bay, he turned to Phil and handed him an envelope.

"Here's yer money, fourteen hundred."

Phil thought to open the envelope and count it but then it came to him, *Well, that'd be purty insulting*, so he undid a button on his shirt and tucked it inside. "I'm much obliged."

"Mcleod says yer not comin' back."

"That's right, I'm not." He paused and then offered up, "The odds ah survivin' this line ah work ain't good."

Harvey nodded in a concerned way. "You may be right." And then he added, "You must be special though. The boss told me to tell ya yer stayin' here tonight – on the house."

Phil laughed. "Yer other suppliers git that?"

"Hell no, like I said, you must be special. Just tell the desk clerk who ya are."

Phil parked his truck on the street not far from the hotel. Off in the distance, he could see the American flag flowing in a gentle westerly breeze. It caused him to recall that he'd driven by a post office on his way there. It may have been because he'd taken to using the mail to communicate with Mcleod or the fact that $1,400.00 was a lot of temptation, but he soon found himself walking in the direction of the flag. By the time he reached the post office, the idea that he was doing the right thing in mailing the money to Catarina had solidified in his mind. The letter sized envelope that Harvey had given him was bulging with bills of various denominations but mostly 20's and a few 100's. There was little doubt as to what it contained. And then the naysayer that always seemed to follow him around shouted out. *With this much money one of these post office fellas could buy himself ah house. It'd be ah real merry Christmas for him this year.* He picked up the envelope from the dark wood counter and started for the glass doors at the front of the post office. He was clicking across the green tile floor mesmerized somewhat by the echo in the high ceiling room when common sense reared up. *Ah fella would have ta be dumber than ah post ta carry around this much cash.* And then the vision of some hoodlum holding him up played in his mind. It stopped him cold just as his hand reached for the door. He sighed, irritated with himself for being indecisive, he went back and purchased a larger manila envelope. With his back to the postal worker's windows he put all of the money but $20 in the envelope, sealed it and addressed it to Catarina. He left the post office feeling as if he had outwitted a fate common to the naïve or unworldly, but not him.

Although his room was free just as Harvey said it would be, there was something odd about the desk clerk's behavior. It was the way he'd said, *Your room has been paid for,* that struck Phil as peculiar. It was a feeling that stayed with him up until the time he got to the room and saw its lavish furnishings. It had thick blue carpet and a big firm bed next to a third story window that looked out over the city. It even had a desk with an electric reading light. But the amenity that impressed him the most was the bathroom. It had a flush toilet and a deep claw foot tub with hot and cold water. At that point, it didn't matter to him who had paid for the room. He took an hour long hot bath allowing his thoughts to become cavalier. *Who says crime doesn't pay?* And then his thoughts turned to fantasy as he wished Catarina were there. But this was short lived as images of Martha repeatedly disrupted how that would've played out. To soak in a tub of deep, hot water was a luxury he'd not known in quite some time. It had been relaxing right up to this point but now he wondered if he wasn't a hypocrite for truly enjoying something that Martha just wanted as a normal part of her life, something that he had taken away from her.

After his bath, he shaved and dressed putting on the other clean shirt that he'd brought. While his room was paid for, his supper was not. A more affordable restaurant was located about four blocks from the hotel. He walked there in a brisk manner as he was hungry. It was not fancy in the least being the proverbial 'hole in the wall'. In a way, it reminded him of the struggling little diner in Baker where he and Catarina had first met Mcleod. His thoughts remained there, with her, throughout his steak supper. By the time he exited the little eatery the waitress had locked the door and turned the open sign to closed. She had even begun putting the chairs upside down on the tables and running a dust mop over the floor. It was almost dark when he stepped outside. The evening was warm and the streets were shadowy and largely deserted. He was pleasantly full and less motivated to walk at a quick pace. He'd just stopped to look at some fly rods in the window of a sporting goods store and was thinking when he had money to spare he'd buy all of the things that he and Catarina would need to go fishing on the Yellowstone River. He was immersed in this daydream, playing a good sized cutthroat trout when a voice behind him said in a threatening tone; "Your name Caldwell?"

Phil turned around; two men, dressed as if they were laborers, both of them a head taller than him and considerably heavier, were standing there. They had apparently gotten out of a car across the street. It was apparent to him their intentions were not friendly. Nonetheless, he owned up to who he was; "I am."

One of the men, the one with a coal black walrus moustache and a flat cap came closer to Phil and glared at him. "It's come to our attention that you've got ah smart mouth." He laughed sarcastically. "We've been hired to help you with that problem."

The threat from Martha's boyfriend earlier that day instantly came to Phil's mind. He shot back; "I'll bet you have since that little weasel bastard is incapable of doing anything about *my problem.*"

And just like that, the fight was on. The man with the flat cap threw a right that he'd telegraphed such that Phil ducked under it and bum rushed the guy. But no sooner had he done this than the other hired goon began landing thunderous blows to the small of Phil's back causing him to let go of the first guy which enabled him to land a haymaker squarely on Phil's nose. The blood came quickly. It was copious, percolating down through Phil's moustache and over his lips, some of it settling in the seams between his teeth so that each tooth was well defined, but it was the excess blood that continued on down his chin and onto his neck being at last absorbed by his only clean shirt that completed the ghoulish picture. Had Phil gone down he might have saved himself further injury but he became enraged and tore into the flat cap man, pummeling him in the face. But, once again, the second goon came to the rescue of the first. He pulled a blackjack from his back pocket. The blow hit Phil just above his right ear. It had the effect of illuminating his mind with the most intense lightning storm he'd ever seen. And then the storm suddenly ended but it was dark and he was being violently jolted, once, twice, three times flat cap man's boot landed in Phil's gut. Their voices were distant and garbled.

"That'll do Gerald. Boyack just wanted him roughed up."

Gerald laughed. "Boyack don't give a shit what happens to this guy. It's this guy's wife that don't want him hurt too bad." And then he knelt beside Phil and began rummaging through his pockets. "Are you shittin' me? Nineteen dollars and twenty cents."

"C'mon, let's git outta here. Somebody just came outta that café up the street."

The goons were long gone by the time the police and the ambulance arrived. Phil told them the men who beat him up had been sent by Marshal Boyack. At that point, the cop asking the questions stopped writing on his notepad. Phil sensed right then and there, he'd get no satisfaction from them. *That little bastard must have some pull in this town.*

Because the bleeding would not stop and his ribs and head ached he accepted a ride in the ambulance to the hospital and that's where he spent the night. The next morning he still had a good sized bump on his head, his nose was swollen and both of his eyes were black but the pain was more tolerable. He left the hospital, having incurred another debt, and began walking to the Front Range Hotel. It was a good ways there which allowed him plenty of time to weigh his options for revenge. However, by the time he reached the hotel, still wearing the white smock the hospital had issued him in lieu of his blood soaked shirt, he had concluded that he had but one choice, go home. Even that might not have been possible had it not been for Harvey and the ten dollars he loaned him. And so it was, late in the afternoon of the following day, he started up the road to Catarina's shanty.

Ranger and Buster began barking when he was a good hundred yards away and that of course prompted Catarina to come outside. Her initial reaction upon seeing that it was Phil's truck was to smile and wave real big. But then, in the next instant, perhaps because the windshield in his truck was gone and the sun was at her back, she began to pick up on the peculiarities of his appearance. It was like dominos falling, her sensing things were not right with him and her smile evaporating as her hand came down to her side. And then, as he came to a stop in front of her, and she could see clearly how he was, more dominos fell. Her heart verily leaped into her throat and the tears pooled, but for an instant before they began to cascade down her face.

Thinking to ease her alarm, Phil did his best to make light of how he looked. He laughed. "My God Catarina, I ain't dead."

She smiled and came back in the same tone. "Land sakes, it appears I can't let you out of my sight without you getting into trouble."

"It kinda appears that way don't it."

Phil slowly eased out of the truck as three of his ribs were cracked. It was as he had imagined and hoped it would be. She stepped close to him and without hesitation kissed him lightly on the lips. And then she moved to his side and put her arm around him, high on his back so as to avoid his ribs. "Let me help you."

He placed his arm across her shoulders. It felt natural and good, like it had been that way for years. They went on for a few steps with the dogs prancing around them when he paused. He did not mean to spoil the moment. It may have been because he was desperate to know her reaction but he looked at her. "I found Martha."

Before he could finish her face suddenly showed disappointment. He savored it for an instant and then went on. "It is over between her and I."

And then she came back. "I'm glad."

EPILOGUE

October 24, 1929 or Black Friday as the newspapers called it changed the lives of a lot of people. For Marshal Boyack, distraught with the stock market crash and the run on his bank which caused it to go under, it was too much. While sitting at his big ornate cherry wood desk in his high back padded chair he put a .32 caliber Colt to his head and pulled the trigger. Unfortunately for him, he suffered for several hours on the floor of his office before the diminutive bullet took effect. It was equally unfortunate, for Martha at least, that with Boyack's passing she was now destitute. She'd made note of this and the fact she'd gotten a job as a hotel maid when she returned a copy of the final divorce papers to Phil. He was tempted to send her a little money but did not. On the other hand, he did pay the bank in Baker a good deal of what he owed, but not all. They were just glad to be receiving money rather than dishing it out.

The lure of easy money, as he referred to it, was too much temptation for Mcleod. He removed his still and the mash containers from Catarina's place and set up operation on some vacant government land thinking that at least that part of it couldn't be tied to him unless the Feds caught him there. But things did not go well and as a repeat offender he was sentenced to a year in the Montana State prison at Deerlodge.

Although it was a gloomy time for the entire country there were some things to celebrate. The little country school that Catarina had been teaching at was going to re-open right after Christmas. It had snowed about six inches, a good moisture start for the coming growing season. And Jack Schneider got released from prison early. Phil sent him the money for a train ticket home and bought all of the things that Ruth Ann and Catarina would need to prepare Christmas dinner. He would have done all of this anyway but this occasion was special, it being he and Catarina's wedding day.

www.ingramcontent.com/pod-product-compliance
Lightning Source LLC
Chambersburg PA
CBHW030740110726
47900CB00008B/2383

* 9 7 8 0 5 7 8 4 5 8 2 3 6 *